Mastermind

By:
Matt Graham

Elite Publishing House
2024

First Edition

Copyright 2024 © Matt Graham/Elite Publishing House

All Rights Reserved

No part of this book may be reproduced or transmitted in any form or by any means, electronic or mechanical, including photocopying, recording or by an information storage and retrieval system – except by a reviewer who may quote brief passages in a review to be printed in a magazine, newspaper or on the Web – without permission in writing from the publisher.

Cover Graphics: Kathryn Denhof
Photo Credit: Matt Graham from his Discovery of Evidence File

To all of those who have found themselves in the nightmare of being wrongfully accused and to those who stood beside me and believed in me during my own personal nightmare.

This is a work of fiction. Unless otherwise indicated, all the names, characters, businesses, places, events and incidents in this book are either the product of the author's imagination or used in a fictitious manner. Any resemblance to actual persons, living or dead, or actual events is purely coincidental. While inspired by real life events, all names and details in this book are fictional.

TABLE OF CONTENTS

PART ONE *11*

PART TWO *194*

PART THREE *278*

EPILOGUE *323*

NOTE FROM THE AUTHOR *325*

ACKNOWLEDGEMENTS *330*

ABOUT THE AUTHOR *331*

Part One
Unforeseen Bewilderment

Chapter One

"Daddy," Amanda screamed as she ran down the sidewalk toward Matt. Her pigtails bounced with each exuberant step, and Matt crouched down in anticipation of her embrace.

"Hi, Baby Girl. How was school?"

"It was great," she cried out against his shoulder in a hug. Then she pulled away and looked at him questionably. "I thought Mama was coming."

"Mama asked me to pick you up today. And guess what else?"

"What?"

"You can spend the night with me tonight."

"Yay," she yelled.

Matt stood and ruffled the top of her hair. "Alright, how about some ice cream before we head home?"

"Double chocolate chip?"

"Anything you want, Baby Girl," Matt said as they walked to his truck.

At the ice cream shop, Matt laughed as ice cream dribbled down Amanda's chocolate-smeared chin. *God, I love her so much*, he thought.

"This is so yummy, Daddy," she squealed.

"Mine's good too," he said with a smile. "So, how was school today? What'd you learn?"

"We're learning about beavers. They use wood to build a dam. And dam isn't a bad word because it's something that stops water, but Robby got in trouble because he was saying it like a bad word instead of like a beaver dam. He said, 'Damn, that's a big beaver, and then the teacher sent him to the principal's office, and I think he got a paddling."

Matt almost spit out his ice cream with his laugh. "Whoa. Well, that's pretty interesting."

"And guess what?"

"What's that?"

"Mrs. Thomas says that beavers mate for life. That means the mommy and daddy stay together forever," she said, still looking down at her ice cream.

"I didn't know that."

"How come you and Mommy can't stay together forever like a beaver?"

"Baby, we've already talked about this. Sometimes mommies and daddies can't get along, and it's better for us to be apart than for you to always see us arguing."

"But I want you to get back together. I want us to all live together again. Besides, Mama's so sad, Daddy. She cries all the time, and she wants you to come home. She told me."

"I don't want you to worry about this stuff, Baby Girl. You're a kid. You're supposed to be focusing on kid stuff like playing ball and learning about beaver dams," he said with a wink. "Listen, I'll always love your mama. She gave me you, and Mama and Daddy love you so much. We'll always try to do what's best for you, okay?"

"Okay," she said. "Will you have a tea party with me when we get home?" she asked, changing the subject abruptly, in true kid fashion.

"Of course."

"And I can dress you up and put makeup on you too?"

Matt feigned a sad look and said, "Makeup, gross. But okay. I guess so."

"Yessss," Amanda said, spewing ice cream across the table in her exuberance.

"But only after you finish your homework."

Later that night, after Matt tucked Amanda into bed, he grabbed a glass of sweet tea from the refrigerator and plopped down on the couch.

Am I doing the right thing? he thought. *I know Shelia wants to get back together, but what's better for Amanda?*

As he wrestled with his emotions, his mind traveled back to the day he told her that he had filed for divorce—one of the most difficult decisions of his life.

"I can't do this anymore, Shelia," Matt said calmly.

"Matt, please. Don't do this. I've already told you. Nothing happened. I swear," Shelia whined.

"It's not just this cop. You know that. This has been coming for a long time. It's everything. Every time I turn around, our friends are telling me how you've been flirting with some new man. It's embarrassing. And all you care about is your image. We never spend time together as a family anymore. It's all about you and your social stuff. If we're not fighting about your flirting, we're fighting about that."

"I don't flirt. I'm just friendly. I'm a sociable person, Matt. You know this."

"It's more than that, and you know it. I've asked you before, but you've never told me what you're not getting from me that you need. You're obviously looking for something that you're lacking in our relationship."

A look of anger flashed over her face. "This is ridiculous..."

"Shelia, this is me. You can be honest with me. Seriously, what do you need from me?"

The anger dissipated. "I don't know," she replied, staring at the floor. "I guess I like to feel wanted."

"And I don't want you? I *chose* to marry you. I *chose* to have a child with you. I've given you everything you ever wanted. You wanted a dress shop? I made it happen. You wanted a bigger house? I started building you one. I don't know what else to do."

"I know. You're right. It's just..."

"Look. We've been through all this before, and honestly, it doesn't even matter at this point. As for the cop, I'll be straight up with you. I don't believe you. I think you've slept with him, but really, I don't even want to know for sure. If you haven't slept with him yet, then you will, eventually. The only thing I can figure out is that you obviously have some self-esteem problems, and if you don't love yourself, I can't make you feel loved. God knows I've been busting my ass trying."

A defiant look crossed her face. "I *do* love myself. I'm freaking amazing, and if you don't appreciate all that I have to offer, someone else will."

"See? That's what I'm talking about. You've threatened this crap for years, and I've just jumped through all the hoops, trying to fill you up, to keep you from walking away. It isn't working. And look around. Look at all this shit in our house. You spend money like a damn billionaire, but none of it is enough. None of it makes you happy."

"You make me happy."

"That's not true, and you know it. Look, I'm just going to be honest with you. I've already talked to an attorney, and I've decided to file for divorce. I love you, but it's just not enough. And I hope we can deal with this like adults, for Amanda's sake."

"What? You met with an attorney? Have you already filed for divorce?" she yelled.

"Shhhh. You're going to wake Amanda up," he said.

"Good. I want to get her up to tell her that her Daddy is ruining our family."

"Calm down, Shelia. I've thought a lot about this, and I think it's the right decision. And as far as Amanda in concerned, we have to be rational about this. We're going to have to talk to her together to make sure she understands that this isn't her fault."

"This *isn't* her fault. It's *your* fault. You're the one who is destroying this family."

"Shelia, we've tried, and it hasn't worked. It's time to move on."

"Maybe you're the one who has a side piece. Are you trying to divorce me so you can go screw a young whore?"

"You know me better than that."

"I don't know you at all. You're a piece of shit, and you don't know what I'm capable of. You're going to regret this."

She walked out that night, slamming the door behind her, and at the time, he believed he was making the right decision.

Later, after the divorce papers arrived, she called him, and her words confirmed that he had done the right thing.

"My family is humiliated. Everyone in town is talking about us getting a divorce. And, of course, everyone assumes that I cheated on you with that stupid cop," she had said.

"I never told anyone about that, Shelia. I would never say anything bad about you. I don't want Amanda hearing anything negative about her mother," he told her.

"Here you go with that high and mighty moral bullshit again, like you're better than me. Well, you're not better. You think because you don't drink and because you go to church, you're superior to me. You might have everyone else fooled, but I know the truth. You're just a third-rate skank with a sorry-ass daddy and an underprivileged mama who can barely make ends meet."

"I thought we were going to try to remain civil for Amanda."

"Amanda deserves better than you. Don't forget that my daddy got you into the trailer business. Everything you have, you owe it to him, and if you want to treat me like this, you better believe that my daddy can take it away."

"I'm not getting into this with you again, Shelia. Just sign the papers. I've given you everything you asked for. You got the house.

"I didn't get the new house."

"The new house isn't even done yet."

"Geez. I can't give you everything. Don't forget you got $300,000 directly from my bank account. What else do you want—my soul?"

"That money won't even touch the loan I took out for my shop, and you know it."

"How is that my fault?" he asked. "You did that behind my back. I had no idea the extent of your debt until this divorce."

"I didn't call you to argue."

"Then why *did* you call?" he asked.

"To tell you that I've decided that I will sign the papers. But I will *also* ruin you. You'll regret the day you decided to piss me off."

Her words had stung. She was angry, and she tried to ruin his reputation in town with her toxic spewing. But he never cared about any of that. She liked the social life—the dinners, the accolades. He only cared about Amanda, and Shelia couldn't erase Amanda's love for her daddy.

After things settled down a bit, Shelia apologized, and these days, they seemed to be doing better at getting along—at least in co-parenting Amanda. He did the right thing at the time. They couldn't have continued like it was going. Their marriage would have imploded.

But now, as he sat alone on a 'visit' with his daughter, he wondered if Shelia had changed. He missed her. Of course, he didn't miss the arguments, but he missed having someone to come home to, someone to talk to, someone to wake up next to in the morning. He sipped his tea and sighed heavily, still lost in conflict.

***

"Hello?" Shelia answered.

"Hey."

"Hey. What's going on?" Shelia asked.

"Ahhh, not much. You know. Same old, same old. Just working," Matt replied.

"Yeah, me too."

"Listen, I want to ask you something."

"Okay."

"What do you think about taking a little trip to Dunedin? Just you and me and Amanda?"

"To Florida? Are you serious?" Shelia asked.

"Yeah."

Shelia was silent for a long pause. "I mean, that would be amazing, but I don't understand what it means. I don't want to get my hopes up about…"

"Shelia, it means we're going to spend some time together. I don't have all the answers, but we have a daughter, and if there's a chance we can work on things, then I have to give it a try."

"That's all I want—another chance."

"I know. I just thought it would be good to get away—you know, see how we do as a family, away from all the opinions and rumblings of everyone around us," Matt said.

"I'd like that, and Amanda will be thrilled."

"Great. Will the week of July 4th work for you?"

"Yep. Definitely."

"Okay. It's a date, and tell Amanda she can bring a friend. Between me and you, I hope she asks Beth."

"Oh gah. Me too. Beth is so sweet. That other kid she met last week is a brat," she said with a hearty laugh.

"This is going to be good," Matt said with a smile.

"Yeah. I'm excited," Shelia replied.

Chapter Two

The drive was long and awkward, as Matt and Shelia forced smiles and made small talk to please Amanda. When they told Amanda about the trip, she was ecstatic, but Matt knew he had to tread carefully. He didn't want to get his daughter's hopes up that they'd get back together. He felt he had a duty to try, though, for her sake, but considering their past failures, Matt was unsure if things would be different the second time around.

When they arrived at the condo, they exhaustedly trudged in, carrying luggage. After they unpacked and plopped down in the living room, Matt clapped his hands and said, "Okay. I know we're all tired, so how about we order a pizza?"

"Sounds good to me," Shelia replied.

"Can we get Papa John's, Daddy?" Amanda asked.

"Of course, Baby. You want pepperoni, right?"

"Can I have a cheese pizza, Mr. Grant?" Beth asked quietly.

Shelia rolled her eyes, and Matt shot her a disapproving look. "Of course, Beth. You can have anything you want, Honey." Matt clapped his hand again. "Two pepperonis and one cheese pizza, coming up. Y'all make yourselves comfortable."

After dinner, the girls settled in bed, watching a silly cartoon movie on Netflix. When Matt and Shelia came in to kiss Amanda goodnight, Shelia ignored Beth. Not wanting her to feel left out, Matt tucked Beth in, too. He smiled, ruffled Beth's hair, and addressed Amanda. "Y'all don't stay up too late, okay? We have a big day of fun tomorrow."

"Okay, Daddy," Amanda said with an innocent smile.

"Thank you, Mr. Grant," Beth cooed.

"And hey, your daddy and I might go take a walk, but we'll just be right out on the beach," Shelia said. "And we won't be gone long. So, stay here in bed. Don't open the door for anyone. Promise me?"

A look of joy crossed Amanda's face, and Matt cringed. *A walk on the beach at night? Yeah. That's definitely gonna get her hopes up that we're getting back together.*

"Okay, Mama," Amanda squealed. "I promise."

They turned off the light, shut the door, and eased out of the room.

Through the door, they heard Beth say, "Your Daddy is sooo nice."

"I know," Amanda said. "He's awesome."

"Your daddy is sooo nice," Shelia mocked in a squealing voice. "Looks like you've got a crush."

"It's not a crush, Shelia. I'm just being nice to her. You act like she's not even here."

"No, I don't. But she's not my daughter. I'm not going to kiss some other woman's kid goodnight."

Matt sighed. "Anyway, a walk on the beach? Isn't that a little presumptuous?"

"We need to talk, and it'll be romantic," Shelia said with a coy smile. "I'll open the wine."

"I don't drink wine," Matt said.

"Well, maybe I can persuade you. It's a special occasion."

Matt sighed again.

***

On the beach, the moon shone down over the water, creating a sparkling effect that rivaled any postcard. It *was* romantic, but Matt wondered if he made a mistake by taking this trip. He didn't want to rush back into a relationship and start the same cycle that ended in their marriage's demise.

When Shelia intimately grabbed his hand, Matt gave her a friendly pat, stopped walking, and said, "Shelia, listen."

"What?" she snapped. "You don't want to hold my hand? Why in the hell did you ask me on this trip if it wasn't to work on us?"

"Hey, hey. Calm down. I *do* want to work on us. I really do. That's why I invited you. I just think we need to work some things out before we rush back in headfirst. I mean, we've ridden this rodeo before, Sheila, and we know how it all ends."

She sighed loudly and dropped his hand. "I know. You're right," she said. "I just love you, and I miss *us*. I miss our family. I want things to go back to the way they used to be."

"The way they used to be wasn't always great. Yeah, we have a lot of good memories, but we fought a lot, and we were both miserable for a long time."

"So, what can I do to convince you that it'll be better—that *I* will be better?"

"I don't need you to convince me. This divorce wasn't all because of you. It was me, too. I know I didn't do everything right. We both ran it off the rails."

"Well, that's not what it looks like to all our friends. Everyone thinks I cheated on you, and that's why we divorced."

"I don't care what other people think, and I don't know why you care either. Look, if this is going to work, we're going to have to be in this together. No finger-pointing. And you know I didn't tell a soul that you cheated on me. I've never said a bad word about you. Whatever happens with us, you're my baby's mama."

"Well, the whole thing's embarrassing. And Daddy is plain pissed. He said he's mortified, and he doesn't know what to say when someone asks about our divorce."

In a moment of sincerity, Matt grabbed Shelia's hand and looked her directly in the eyes. "I love you. I've always loved you. That has never changed. But this stuff, the problems you and I had in the past, it's above my paygrade. I don't know how to fix it so we don't make the same mistakes again. So, I've been thinking. Maybe we can see a marriage counselor. I know we're technically not married anymore, but I think we owe it to Amanda to do it right if we're going to try again. And maybe it'll help."

"Marriage counseling? Daddy probably wouldn't like that either. He doesn't believe in therapy."

Matt dropped her hand. "You're a grown-ass woman, Shelia. You don't need your Daddy's permission to do what's best for your life. I'm trying to do the right thing here, but you have to meet me half way."

"No, you're right. I want you in my life, Matt," Shelia said, grabbing his hand again. "Amanda adores you, and so do I. If you think marriage counseling will help, then I'll do it."

Matt felt relieved, and still holding her hand, he turned and looked out over the lunar-illuminated ocean. "It really is beautiful here, isn't it?"

"It is. And being here with you only makes it more beautiful." She reached up to his face, physically turning his eyes toward her. "I love you, Matt, and I'll do anything to show you that."

In that moment, with the sound of the waves crashing around them and the soft sand under his feet, he believed her. He swallowed hard as hope crawled up from his stomach into his heart.

"I love you too," he said as he leaned down and kissed her.

***

The next morning, Matt eased the door open and tiptoed through the kitchen to make coffee. He didn't want Amanda to know that he and Shelia slept in the same room the night before. Though he hoped marriage counseling would help, he still wasn't ready to declare their marriage renewed to Amanda.

"Hi, Mr. Grant," Beth said.

Matt whirled around and saw Beth and Amanda coming in from the patio door.

"Jesus. Y'all scared me. What're you doing up so early?" Matt asked.

"We were out on the patio feeding the seagulls, Daddy," Amanda said.

"I don't think you're supposed to do that, but it's fine." Matt smiled at his daughter. "I'm going to make some coffee for your mom. Y'all need anything? We have some cereal."

"I'm not really hungry," Beth said.

"I am," Amanda said with a smile.

"Okay, Amanda. Well, grab some Cheerios for now, but don't eat too much. Don't want you to get full. We'll go get breakfast when Mama gets up," Matt said, looking at Amanda.

"Oooh, pancakes," Amanda squealed.

Beth grabbed Amanda's arm and pulled her to their room. "Come on. I have some new lip gloss you'll love, and Mama bought me a highlighter pallet."

And just like that, Amanda wasn't hungry anymore. Matt laughed. "Just a little makeup..." Matt yelled.

"What Daddy?" she asked.

"Never mind. Have fun," he said, starting the coffee.

When the coffee was finally done, Matt poured a cup to take to Shelia when he heard footsteps behind him.

"Good morning," Shelia said with a smile and a kiss on the cheek.

"Perfect timing," he said, holding up her coffee cup.

"I smelled it. What'd I miss?" she asked.

"The girls were feeding the seagulls off the balcony, and now they're putting on makeup."

"Oh, my Lord. That should be interesting," she said with a laugh.

"So... last night. It was nice," Matt said.

Shelia turned around with a mischievous smile. "It was more than nice. It was naughty *and* nice," she said as she rubbed his arm.

"I still think..." Matt started.

"Let me stop you right there," Shelia interrupted. "We love each other, and we did nothing wrong. This doesn't have to be awkward. We've both agreed to go to marriage counseling when we get back, and we'll just go from there."

"You're right," Matt said.

"I just know how you over-analyze everything. Just let it go. Take some time off from your mental scrutiny, and let's just enjoy the week, okay?"

"Alright," Matt said with a smile. "I just..."

"Let it goooooo... Let it gooooo," Shelia sang.

Matt laughed. "Oh God. You know I hate that song. If I never hear another Elsa quote again, I'll be a happy man."

Shelia smiled. "Join me on the patio for some expert people-watching?" she asked.

"I'm right behind you," Matt said, patting her bottom.

He felt so happy, he couldn't help himself.

Chapter Three

The next day, they visited Fun Factory. As promised, Matt kept the conversation light-hearted and focused on leisure instead of overthinking the trajectory of their relationship. And Shelia was right. Simply focusing on being together was great for Amanda. Matt was happy to see her endless laughs and smiles.

After riding multiple roller coasters, Matt felt queasy, even though his stomach was rumbling from hunger.

"Babe, you okay? You're kinda looking green," Shelia said.

"That spinning contraption bout' threw me over the edge," he said. "But I'm hungry. Y'all ready to get outta here and go get something to eat?" he asked the girls.

"Whatever you wanna do, Daddy," Amanda said with a beaming smile.

"Waiit," Beth squealed. "We haven't even been on the bumper cars yet."

"I forgot about the bumper cars. Can we please just ride them once, Daddy? Then we can go," Amanda pleaded in her most angelic voice.

"Yeah, Daddy," Shelia said with a playful smile. "Can we ride the bumper cars?"

Always a sucker, Matt conceded. "Bumper cars. Then, we have to get some real food."

"Good. I'm going to go really fast," Beth yelled and started jogging toward the bumper car exhibit.

Shelia looked at Matt and rolled her eyes again. "Lord, help me have some patience with these children," she said. Then, she yelled out, "Beth, slow down. Wait on us." She turned to Matt, "Speaking of people talking about me. Can you imagine what people would say if I lost a child in Florida?"

"Yeah. That would be bad. She slowed down, though," Matt said, pointing to the girls ahead of them. Then, as they sped up to catch up with the kids, he grabbed Shelia's hand.

"Hold up now." Shelia gave a short laugh. "I think you're moving too fast for me. Don't you want to talk about our relationship some more before we make the big choice to hold hands in public?" she asked, her voice dripping in sarcasm.

"Oh, shut up," Matt said with a smile.

***

At the restaurant, Matt ordered soup and salad, hoping the light meal would give his stomach some relief. The accompanying ladies ordered a seafood medley, including shrimp, oysters, fish, and crabs. The conversation remained lighthearted, and they enjoyed the entire meal without any awkward moments. While waiting for the waitress to bring their check, Shelia's phone rang.

"Hello? What? Calm down, Mama. Hang on. I can't hear you." She turned to Matt and said, "I'm going outside so I can hear."

Matt nodded, a worried expression crossing his face.

"What's wrong, Daddy?" Amanda asked, her child's intuition honing in on his anxious aura.

"I don't know, Baby Girl. It sounds like that was Nonna on the phone. I'm sure everything's okay, though," he said in his most convincing voice.

The restaurant was busy, and their waitress was obviously inundated with patrons, but Matt was anxious to pay for the check and figure out what was going on with his in-laws—*my ex-in-laws*, he thought to himself. Had he really started thinking of their relationship like a marriage again in a matter of a few days? He shook the thought off and grabbed the nearest apron-wearing server.

"Hey, can you see if you can find our waitress? We need our checks. I think her name was Trisha."

"Absolutely, sir," the bleach-blonde waitress said with a forced smile.

After what seemed like an eternity, Matt paid for the meal and ushered the girls outside. He found Shelia in the parking lot beside his SUV, still on the phone. He could tell that she had been crying.

"Okay, Mama... Okay. I'm sorry this happened... I know. Okay... I love you, too. Bye."

"What's going on?" Matt immediately asked. "Are you okay?"

"Damn it," Shelia said. Then she glanced at Amanda and Beth. "That's a bad word. Don't use that word." Addressing Matt again, she told him, "Someone broke into Mama and Daddy's house. They got in the safe and cleared it out."

"Oh, my Lord," Matt said. "What are they gonna do? They gonna end their vacation?"

"Mama says Daddy wants to stay—that there's nothing he can do about it now, anyway."

"Well, that's nuts. Somebody needs to be there to check it out. They need to make sure the house is locked up. I'll call him later and offer to fly him home on a personal jet. Sam owes me a favor, so I bet he'll work them in and make sure they can get home immediately. Are you all right? You look upset."

"Not really. Daddy had cash in that safe. It was supposed to be for my inheritance—and for Amanda. Now, it's all gone. Every last cent."

"I remember William talking about his safe. How much money did it have in it?" Matt asked.

"A lot," Shelia said. "I mean, I don't know for sure, but knowing Daddy, there's no telling. Mama just said that it was his 'life savings.' But Mama didn't even sound that upset. I can't figure out why they're being so nonchalant about all this. Mama said, 'It's just money.' I said the same thing you did—about them coming home, but she said Daddy won't budge—that it's his dream vacation, and he's not ending it."

"Let's go back to the condo, and I'll call William myself. Maybe he'll listen to me," Matt said.

Amanda, still standing by the truck, asked, "Who stole from Nonna and Pop?"

Shelia, seemingly snapping out of her reverie, looked at Amanda. "I don't know, Baby, but Nonna and Pop are still in Colorado, so they're safe, and that's all that matters. Did you enjoy your lunch?" she asked, trying to change the subject.

"Yep. It was deeee-lish," she replied with a smile.

"The fish was stinky," Beth said.

"Of course it was, Beth," Shelia said, rolling her eyes at Beth again.

"No, you're stinky," Matt said with a laugh, and he ruffled Beth's hair, which elicited a big laugh from the girls.

"Your daddy is funny," Beth said to Amanda.

"Yep. He's hilarious. Now, get in the truck," Shelia announced. "We're going back to the condo." As she opened the truck door, she addressed Matt. "Mama needs a drink."

***

Back at the condo, Shelia settled the girls in their bedroom and put a movie on the television. Then, she made a Tom Collins and asked Matt, "You sure you don't want a drink?"

"Nah. I'll just drink my sweet tea. You're starting kinda early," he replied.

"Well, we're on vacation. When in Rome…"

"Let me call your daddy," Matt said, cutting her off. From his cell phone, Matt clicked William's contact information.

"Hello?"

"Hey, William. It's Matt."

"Hey. How's the trip going?"

"It's been great 'til today when we got that shocking news. How y'all holding up?"

"It's a damn shame. That's for sure. Sons of bitches broke the door down and ripped the door to the safe right off."

"Crap. So, the police called you?" Matt asked.

"Yep. Sheriff. Tommy Tucker. He and I are friends from way back. Said he's gonna put his best men on this."

"Well, that's good. Listen, my buddy has a personal jet, and he owes me a favor. I can get you a jet there today or in the morning, and he can fly y'all home. I'll take care of the whole thing."

"I ain't leaving Colorado, Matt," William said.

"Why? Don't you want to go check everything out—at least to make sure they didn't take any other stuff? Did he say the house was ransacked?"

"Naw. He said everything looked normal except for the safe. Hell, I've already lost my life savings, and I've already paid for this hotel. I'm not losing any more money on this crap, and like I said, I can't help what has already happened. I might as well just enjoy what's left of our trip."

"What about the door? You said they broke the door down."

"The sheriff said he'd board it up."

Well, Shelia and I were only planning to stay a few more days, anyway. I guess we could go back early. You want us to go home and check it out?"

"That's your call. I'm not going to tell anyone to cut their trip short, but it would make Diana feel better if Shelia got over there and talked to Tommy. She tried to sound strong on the phone with Shelia, but she's a little shook up over this, somebody being in our house and all."

"Okay. I'll talk to Shelia about it. Honestly, Shelia's pretty upset, and I don't know if she'd even be able to enjoy a few more days here, especially knowing y'all aren't coming home."

"Alright then. Just let me know what y'all decide..." There was a moment of silence before William spoke again. "How're things going in the romance department?"

Matt gave a short laugh. "I don't think Shelia would appreciate me discussing our love life with you, William."

"Well, I don't give a damn what Shelia would appreciate, to be honest. The both of y'all embarrassed me with this divorce crap—all these rumors flying around. People don't even want to look me in the eye anymore."

"It's the 21st century, William. People get divorced. Sometimes they get back together. Sometimes they don't. I really doubt your crowd is that concerned about our marriage."

"Well, all I know is, you hurt my daughter. I swear she cried for a solid month. And putting Amanda through all that? You should be ashamed of yourself. Real men stick it out. Divorce. That's a bunch of bullshit. Only pussy men let their wives go. Back in my day, if you had a problem in your marriage, you learned to grin and bear it. But, like this robbery, what's done is done. Y'all got your divorce, and that shoulda been it. So, I'm not ashamed to tell you that I advised Shelia to let it go—to let you go. No need starting the whole damn process over again. You ended it, so it should end. And, of course, she didn't listen to me because there y'all are—on vacation, like nothing ever happened. I ain't happy about this situation, and I sure as hell don't like her being on vacation with you."

"Well, that's your opinion, William. But I don't think now is the time to have this conversation. Besides, this is a decision Shelia and I have to make. With all due respect, it's none of your business."

"The hell it ain't. We're talking about *my* daughter and *my* granddaughter here. I've got a duty to protect them from everything that'll hurt them—and that includes you. And you better believe I'll do whatever it takes to safeguard them. Now, I let Shelia go on this little trip with you because she was so adamant about it, but you know it, and I know it.

I can put my foot down and stop this whole thing anytime I want to."

"You *let* her go on this trip? Jesus, William, you're talking about her like she's a child. Anyway, I don't want to get into this with you. I just called to make sure y'all were all right and to offer to fly you home. The offer still stands. Let me know if you change your mind."

"I won't change my mind. Thanks for the call," William said and hung up the phone.

Matt stared at his phone a moment before putting it down and shaking his head. Shelia came in from the balcony, and as she made a new drink in the kitchen, she asked, "Well? How'd it go?"

"He's not going home, but he said it would make your mama feel better if you went home and talked to the sheriff."

"I was thinking about that outside on the patio. Maybe we *should* go home early."

"Whatever," Matt said coldly. "Whatever you wanna do."

"Hey. What's the attitude?" Shelia asked sharply.

"Nothing. It's just that... well, your daddy made it very clear that he doesn't want us getting back together. He said he told you not to go on this trip with me, too."

Shelia shook her head and took a big drink of her Tom Collins. "That's just Daddy ranting. He likes to rant."

"I thought I had a pretty good relationship with William. I had no idea he hated me so much."

"He doesn't hate you. He just likes to control everything, and he has this macho-man mentality. You filed for divorce, so he wants me to shut you out completely. But I couldn't do that."

"You never told me he was telling you stuff like that."

"Well, you know I want you back, and we already had enough obstacles in our way. I just didn't want you to have to worry about Daddy. He shouldn't be a factor in whether we get back together."

"We definitely agree on that, but you have to quit letting him treat you like a child. He still controls you, and I'm no expert, but that doesn't seem very healthy."

"Whatever. What'd he say about the break-in?"

"Said they broke into the front door and ripped the door of the safe off. Sheriff called him. Other than that, he seemed pretty indifferent about it."

"That's what I thought, too. But seriously, I think we should go home. I don't want to ruin our trip, but somebody should at least be there to talk to the police and make sure they're trying to catch the scumbag that did this."

"I know. You're right. I told William that I didn't think you'd enjoy the rest of the trip anyway after all this."

She walked up to Matt and put her nose nearly to his. He smelled gin, and her voice came out slow and methodical. "Hey. Us leaving has nothing to do with you and me. Every second with you here has been perfect. And Daddy doesn't make my decisions for me. We're going back to take care of business, but that doesn't change what has happened between us. Okay?"

"Okay," Matt said, but the ecstatic thrill of hope he felt the day before had already stared to dwindle.

Chapter Four

"Daddy, do I have to go to this family reunion?" Amanda squealed.

"Yep. I'm sorry, Baby Girl. It's important to your mamma—and to Nonna and Pop. They have family coming from all over, and they want everyone to see how sweet and beautiful you are."

"I don't know why I can't just skip it and stay with you one more night."

"Sweetie, I know it's hard, and every time I'm away from you, I miss you like crazy, but this is just the way it has to be right now. And I'll see you again this weekend. Haven't you ever heard the saying, 'Absence makes a heart grow fonder'?"

"No. What does it mean?"

"It means, when you're away from someone, you miss them. Then, when you get to see them, being with them is even better because you missed them so much."

"I don't like that saying," Amanda replied with a sigh.

Matt chuckled. "That's okay. Besides, you'll have fun playing with your cousins," he said as he pulled into the park. "There's your Pop right there. I know he'll be happy to see you. Go give him a big hug."

Amanda bounded out of the truck and ran into William's arms as Matt exited the vehicle. He inhaled deeply and prepared himself for his first encounter with William since their squabble on the phone in Florida.

"Hey William," Matt said, holding his hand out for a shake.

"Matt," William said, grabbing his hand.

"Amanda, go play with your cousins, Baby. I'll come tell you goodbye before I leave," Matt said.

"Okay, Daddy," Amanda yelled as she ran toward the pavilion.

"Any news on the break-in?" Matt asked.

"Nothing yet, but it's still pretty early in the investigation. We had a storm while we were on vacation, too, and it looks like we're going to need a new roof. You know, when it rains, it pours."

"I hear you," Matt said.

"Thinking about one of those metal roofs. I can get a good deal on the supplies. Just need someone to install it. The wife says I'm too old to crawl up on the roof. So, I'd like to do it myself, but you know how it goes. 'Happy wife, happy life.'"

"My buddy Eric sells metal shingles, and he has a crew that installs them too. I can give him a call."

"I'd appreciate that, Matt. Send him out to my house for a quote. If he can beat my guy's price on the shingles, I'll buy those from him too."

"Good deal. I'll call him tomorrow morning." After a moment of awkward silence, Matt said, "All right. I better go tell Amanda bye and let y'all get on with the reunion. Good to see you, William."

"You too, Matt," William said, and he shook Matt's hand again.

As Matt went to find Amanda, he thought to himself, *that was kind of awkward.*

***

"Hey, Eric. It's Matt."

"Hey, buddy. How you doing?"

"I'm good, Man. Thanks. How 'bout you?"

"Not bad. Busy with work, as usual."

"That's good. I called to give you some more work. My father-in-law wants to put in a metal roof. So, I was going to see if you could go out there and give him a quote."

"William?" Eric asked.

"Yep."

"Listen, Matt. This is none of my business, but I was going to call you today, anyway. You know how small this town is, so I heard William's house was broken into."

"Yeah. Stole a lot of money."

"Well, a friend of mine hangs out with William, and according to my buddy, William thinks *you* did it," Eric said.

"Wait. What? That doesn't make any sense. William knows I was in Florida with Shelia when the break-in happened."

"I'm just telling you what I heard. And it's all over town because my wife came home yesterday and told me the same thing."

"That's nuts. There's no way they can think I did this," Matt said.

"I thought it was crazy, too. That's why I was gonna give you a call today, but if I were you, I wouldn't be doing any favors for William Carson anytime soon."

"You're right about that. Cancel that quote until I get this crap figured out."

"I've got your back, Buddy. Anybody that disrespects of friend of mine won't be my client. Anyway, you know I don't buy into all the gossip stuff, but I thought you should know. If you need anything, let me know."

"Thanks, Eric."

***

"C'est la Vie Boutique. This is Shelia."

"Hey. It's me."

"Hey, Hon. What's up?"

"I just got off the phone with Eric. He said he heard your daddy thinks I had something to do with the break-in."

"Eric Jones? Please. He's just gossiping. I wouldn't worry about it."

"Well, I don't want my name associated with that crap."

"Seriously, don't worry about it, Matt. Claire and I think Mickey Tharpe did it."

"Your sister, Claire?"

"Yeah. Mickey had been hanging out with Daddy at the house a lot, and Claire said he knew about the safe and that it had a lot of money in it."

"Well, a lot of people knew about the safe. Your daddy kind of likes to brag."

"Yeah, but Claire said that Mickey's wife threw him out. Then, he was arrested for sexual harassment, and after that, the FBI got involved."

"The FBI? For what?"

"Heck if I know, but supposedly, his bank accounts were frozen, so if anyone needed the money, it was him."

"What's your daddy think about all this?"

"I don't know. He's been pretty quiet about it to me."

"Okay. Well, changing the subject, the doctor's office called and said you didn't show up for your individual therapy session. I thought we agreed on trying counseling."

"I just couldn't do it, Matt. I thought we were going to couples counseling—not individual counseling."

"I already told you. You meet with them individually at first; then, they'll bring us in together."

"Look, I don't need to see a shrink. I'm not crazy. Besides, I don't really think we need counseling. Everything was perfect in Florida."

"We talked about this. We can't just get back together and repeat the same cycle."

"It's *not* the same cycle. It's different. *I'm* different, Matt."

"You can't change if you don't know your reasoning for doing something in the first place. Why did you cheat on me?"

"I'm not talking about this bullshit, Matt."

"Well, if you don't know *why* you did it, then you'll do it again. And if I don't know what I was doing to make you unhappy, then I'll do the same thing again."

"I don't want to talk about the past. If we're going to start over, then we have to focus on the future. And don't forget, you were with other women, too."

"Yeah, I was with other women when we separated—and after we divorced. I'm just saying, if you don't know what caused you to go outside of our marriage, then it'll happen again. That's what therapy is for. It doesn't mean you're crazy. It's just getting help to figure some stuff out. I need it, too. I went to my individual session. This is important, Shelia. If we start over, then I have to make sure that *my* behavior doesn't drive you to another man's bed."

"Well, I changed my mind about it. I'm not doing it. We can talk it out ourselves. I don't need some stupid ass woman prying into my damn business and telling my personal shit to everyone in town."

"That wouldn't happen. There's a client-patient privilege."

"Whatever. Like that means anything in this town."

"I won't do it, Shelia."

"Won't do what?"

"If you don't agree to go to therapy, then this is over—*we're* over. I can't keep repeating this same cycle."

"What the fuck, Matt? Just like that, you're giving up on us?"

"I'm not the one giving up. I want us to work on it—with professional help."

"Whatever. I don't give a shit anymore. It's your fucking loss."

"Shelia..." Matt tried to reason with her, but she had already hung up the phone.

***

Matt walked into the sheriff's station, and he clenched his fist with nervousness. *Relax,* he told himself. *You're just going in to give a statement.*

"May I help you?" the receptionist asked.

"Yeah. I'm Matt Grant. I'm William Carson's son-in-law. I was going to come in and make a statement about his recent break-in."

"Have a seat," she said without looking up from her computer. "I'll let the detective on the case know you're here."

Matt sat down on the hard bench outside and glanced at the receptionist behind the glass window. She picked up the phone and murmured some words he couldn't hear. Within minutes, a gigantic man in a sheriff's uniform came into the waiting room.

"Mr. Grant?" he asked.

Matt stood and wiped his hand on his pants before extending it to the officer. "Yes, sir," he said.

"I'm Sheriff Tommy Tucker."

"Matt Grant," he said, squeezing the sheriff's hand.

"Come on back, and we'll get you fixed up."

Matt followed the sheriff behind the door. *Why is the sheriff talking to me? The receptionist said she'd let the detective know. Does the sheriff take all the statements?* He followed the officer, trying to ignore his trepidation.

The sheriff opened a door to a dark room and pointed at a chair beside a small table. "Have a seat. Would you like something to drink? Coffee? Water?"

"No, I'm good. Thank you," Matt said.

"Okay. Let me go get the file, and I'll be right back," Sheriff Tucker said.

He shut the door when he left, and the thud of the doorjamb echoed in the room, sending a spark of doom through Matt's stomach. *This is an interrogation room. Why in the hell did I come here? Calm down,* he told himself.

In minutes, the sheriff returned, holding a folder. He sat down across from Matt and smiled at him over the small table. "Okay. My secretary said you're here to give a statement regarding William Carson's break-in."

"Yes, sir. I'm William's son-in-law... well, ex-son-in-law. If I can do anything to help, then I'm happy to do it."

"Well, I appreciate that, Matt. Can I call you Matt?"

"Of course."

"How's your relationship with William? Y'all get along?" the sheriff asked.

"It's all right, I reckon," Matt said. "When I was married to Shelia, we had a great relationship. Things feel a little off now that we're divorced, but we stay pretty cordial for my daughter's sake."

"So, you wouldn't say you hate him?"

"Hate him? No. What's this about? Look, I'm going to be straight with you. A buddy of mine heard through the grapevine that some people think I had something to do with this. That's why I'm here. I just want to set the record straight."

"Well, we appreciate that clarification, Matt. May I ask where you were the night of the burglary?"

"I was in Florida—with Shelia and our daughter, Amanda. William knows that."

"So, what was the nature of the trip? When did you plan it?"

"With all due respect, sir, the nature of my trip is none of your business." Matt paused and took a breath. "But if you must know, Shelia and I were considering reconciling, and I thought it'd be a good idea to get away—to spend some time together as a family."

"So, you planned the trip?"

"Yeah. I planned it. So what?"

"Well, if you arranged the break-in, then it would make sense for you to plan an out-of-state trip to be away when the burglary occurred."

"Arranged it? What's that supposed to mean?"

"It doesn't mean anything yet, Matt. We're just covering all angles here."

"I had nothing to do with this."

"Well, if that's true, then I don't think you'd have a problem taking a lie-detector test. Our technician is here today, as a matter of fact."

"I'll take it right now."

"Great. I'll make the arrangements. Now, regarding your official statement, you claim that you were in Florida and that you have no knowledge on who perpetrated this act?"

"That's right."

"What about the safe? Did you know about the safe?"

"Yeah, I knew about the safe, but so did everyone who ever went to William's house. He always bragged about that safe and how much damn money he had."

"Okay. Thank you. Wait right here. I'll bring you the paperwork to write out an official statement, and we'll get the lie-detector-technician ready. Thank you for coming in, Matt."

His words dripped with southern hospitality, but Matt didn't trust him. In his gut, he knew that the sheriff was a snake—a common serpent, trying to get Matt to say something incriminating. Matt looked around the room and saw his reflection in the mirrored window to his left. He looked pale, and he saw beads of sweat on his forehead. *Jesus. I look guilty. And they're watching me right now.* He wiped the sweat from his palms and took a deep breath. *They're just covering their bases. It's okay. The lie detector will prove that this is all bullshit.*

When the door opened again, the sound erupted out of the silence, startling Matt into a nervous jump.

"Let's do the lie detector first, and afterward, you can write out a statement. That okay with you, Buddy?" the serpent asked with a greasy smile.

"Let's do it," Matt replied.

***

Sitting in his truck in the police parking lot, Matt breathed deeply, trying to calm his racing heart. With shaking hands, he picked up his cell phone and called Shelia.

"What do you want, Matt?" she immediately said.

"I just went to the police station to give my statement, and they think I planned William's break-in."

"Yeah, so?"

"So? Shelia, you know I didn't have anything to do with this."

"Do I?"

"Of course you do. You know me. You know I wouldn't do something like this."

"I *thought* I knew you, Matt. I mean, honestly, I thought the trip to Florida was a chance for us to get back together, but now I know that you just needed an alibi for this break-in."

"Shelia, you can't be serious. Florida was amazing. We really connected, and I thought it was the beginning of us getting back together. That was real."

"Yeah, and as soon as we got back, you threw it all away because I wouldn't go to your precious therapist."

"I told you that you could pick another therapist, Shelia."

"That's not the point. Look. Yeah, Florida was great, but it was just sex, Matt. And I can't be involved with a criminal. Honestly, maybe I don't know you at all, and if that's true, then I'm not sure you need to be around Amanda."

"Shelia…"

"I'm done talking, Matt. Don't call me again," Shelia said and hung up.

***

Matt paced between his kitchen and living room, talking to himself aloud.

"What the heck is going on? Why in the heck would anyone think I did this? It has to be William ranting again. He's just mad because Shelia and I were thinking about getting back together. This is his way to stop it. Damn it. Now, everybody in town wonders if I had something to do with this crap. So what? Who cares?"

He wrung his hands through his hair and grabbed a bottle of water from the fridge.

"There's no telling what they're saying to Amanda. Poor thing. And Shelia? She believes this crap, just like that? Well, that settles that. We're done. I can't be in a relationship with someone who doesn't trust me. 'It was just sex, Matt.' What the hell? I should've known all that talk about working on our relationship was a ruse. Just sex.

Hell, that's all she cares about. Sex. And she can get that from anybody. Well, go get it, Shelia."

He slammed his hand against the counter.

"And after all I've done for her. Bought her everything she ever wanted. Forgave her over and over. Hell, she probably slept with damn near every man in town. *She* was embarrassed by the divorce? I'm freaking embarrassed, Shelia. I'm the one who looks like a damn idiot, coming back to you over and over while you screw around. And now your family's gonna try to pin a burglary on me? Good luck with that. There's no evidence because it's not true. They think they're so damn important. You're not in the mafia, William."

Matt took a long swig of water and inhaled deeply. He had to get all his venting out before Shelia brought Amanda by for the weekend. He hadn't talked to Shelia since she accused him of the burglary, but she texted him, saying she'd bring Amanda for their regular visitation. At least he was going to get to spend the weekend with Amanda.

Damn it, Shelia. Why in the hell would you believe this crap?

Despite how he felt about Shelia at this point, he refused to say anything negative to Amanda about her mother. None of this was Amanda's fault.

Chapter Five

The next morning, Matt rolled out of bed, weary after a night of restless sleep. He went to the sink, brushed his teeth, and splashed water on his face.

"Get it together, Matt," he said to himself. "You know you didn't do this, and you live in the freaking United States of America, where justice prevails. The truth will all come out, and years later, you'll laugh about all this stress."

He plodded into the kitchen and opened the fridge. Deciding to make breakfast, he pulled out bacon and eggs. Just as he was cracking eggs in a bowl, the doorbell rang. He glanced at his watch—7:00 a.m. *Who would be here so early?* he thought.

When he opened the door, his eyes shot open wide in surprise. "Shelia. What're you doing here?"

"Wow," she said with a coy smile. "I'm actually surprised you're here. Aren't you usually already at work at this time?"

"I've been a little stressed out," Matt said, running his hands through his hair. "Decided to take it easy today. Anyway, you didn't answer my question. What're you doing here?"

She smiled again and shifted her legs nervously. "I just wanted to see you. Gosh, I forgot how good you look when you wake up, with your hair all messed up, and in pajama pants."

"Look—" Matt started.

"Can I come in?" she interrupted him.

Matt exhaled loudly and opened the door wide so she could enter. "I'm making breakfast. Are you hungry?" he asked.

"Sure. That'd be great," she said, and she waltzed into the living room and plopped down on the couch.

Matt returned to his eggs and blew out another deep exhale before addressing her. "I'm actually glad you came by. We need to talk about this break-in crap."

"Yeah. We do," she said. "Did you do it?"

Matt froze and slammed his hand on the counter. "That's enough. Stop accusing me of something you know I didn't do. I'm not capable of doing something so horrible."

Shelia stood and walked toward the kitchen so she could look him in the eyes. "We're all capable of doing horrible things, Matt. It's human nature." Then she smiled. "Man. I almost forgot how sexy you are when you're mad."

"Are you seriously coming on to me right now?" Matt asked. "This is serious, Shelia. I don't want you putting any ideas into Amanda's head. Surely to God you haven't insinuated that I had something to with this around her."

Her smile disappeared. "I think she has a right to know who her father is."

Matt set the whisk down on the counter and walked closer to Shelia.

"Ooh. Use a spoon rest. You're getting raw eggs on the countertop," Shelia said curtly.

"I'm sick of this shit," Matt said.

Shelia laughed. "Oh, you must be pissed. Mr. Holy said a cuss word. Now, I'm *sure* you did it. If you can throw all your morals out the window and start cussing like that, then a little robbery would've been no sweat off your back."

She was obviously joking, as she was laughing, but at that moment, Matt envisioned slapping her—hard. He sucked in a deep breath through his nose. "I don't give a damn what you think about me—or what you say about me, but you will *not* poison *my* daughter with your lies. Around her, keep my name out of your damn mouth."

Shelia took a step closer, where her nose almost touched his. "Or what?" she asked. "Are you going to hit me?"

Matt remained silent, still.

"You want to hit me now? Don't you?"

Just as Matt was about to back away, Shelia grabbed him and kissed him, deep and hard. He was so flabbergasted, he didn't move, but then, in an instant, all the stress melted away. In her kiss, he remembered the day he married her—beautiful and caring. He thought about their family—he and Shelia and Amanda, and he yearned to go back—back to a time before he knew about her sexual proclivities, a time when everything wasn't about money and status and who was right, who was smarter, who was a better person.

He kissed her back, and when she whispered, "Take me to the bedroom," he found himself in a trance, as if he were a genie, granting her every wish. She wrapped her legs around him, and he carried her down the hall.

In the bedroom, he placed her gently on the bed and stepped back, trying to regain his logic, but then she ripped off her shirt, and Matt gasped at her boldness. Almost methodically, he stepped toward her, but she held up a hand.

"Wait. Let's record it—like we used to," she said.

"I don't think that's a good idea. We're not married anymore, and…"

"Quit being so damn good," Shelia said. "I want to see your bad side. I know it's in there."

Matt shook his head, and before he knew it, he was setting up the camcorder to record, focused on the bed.

When Matt returned to her, she immediately kissed him again, casting another spell, and he was hypnotized by her embrace. Suddenly, she pulled back and looked into his eyes. Then, she gritted her teeth. "Hit me, Matt. Hit me."

Matt's eyes widened. "I can't, Shelia. I can't. I wouldn't—"

"I want it rough," she said. "I want it to hurt so good."

He couldn't hit her—he could never do that, but her words emblazoned a fire in his soul, and as he flipped her over roughly, he thought, *causing her a little pain wouldn't be too bad.*

***

Later, an awkward silence filled the room as they sipped their coffee and munched on the breakfast that Matt was finally able to make.

"You going to the boutique today?" Matt asked, piercing the silence.

"Yep. After lunch," Shelia replied.

"I might take the whole day off," Matt said.

"That's good," Shelia said, munching on a piece of bacon. "Don't forget you have to pick up Amanda from school tomorrow."

"I know. More coffee?" Matt asked. When she nodded, he took her cup to the coffee pot. "Look, Shelia," he said, with his back turned, filling her coffee cup. "That was..."

"Amazing?" she asked.

"Yeah," Matt replied. "But I don't know what it means for us. We keep going in circles, and—"

"Stop, Matt. Just stop. It doesn't mean anything. It was sex—just sex. Yeah, it was great sex, but you don't have to overanalyze every little thing. Geez."

He handed her the coffee and sat down at the table. "Yeah, but that's the thing. I don't want to be a booty-call. You're the mother of my child—and most of the time, in my mind, you're still my wife. I love you, and letting you go has been one of the hardest things I've ever done. And just when I think I'm moving on, you reel me back in."

"I just missed you, okay? It's not that big of a deal, and it doesn't have to happen again," she said.

Silence filled the room again. Matt's stomach clenched, and he pushed his plate back, frustrated at the constant unsettling feeling he experienced around her. "Okay, well, back to the robbery situation..."

"Oh, God. Not this again," Shelia said.

"Jesus, Shelia. This robbery is a big deal, and I don't want Amanda to think of her father as someone who could do something like that—and you *know* me. I don't understand why you'd even entertain the idea of me being a part of this—much less let Amanda consider it."

She huffed. "Can I be real with you?"

"Please," Matt said in a pleading voice.

"Daddy thinks you orchestrated this whole thing. And yeah, I know you, so my first thought was that you'd never do something like this—but I've known my Daddy longer, and he's pretty convincing—he's positive that the trip to Florida was just a ploy, an alibi, and then, when we got back, you shut me out, saying that we couldn't get back together, so that made me think that maybe it *was* just a trip for your own convenience."

"I told you I wanted to get counseling, and you refused to go—that's why we didn't get back together."

"Excuses, excuses. It's all rather convenient," she said.

Matt huffed. "Okay, so, hypothetically speaking, I asked you to go to Florida and had someone break into your father's house while we were gone, stealing his life-savings. Then, I brush you off, ending the possibility of us getting back together. And yet, you still come over here and seduce me? You're telling me that you don't mind sleeping with someone who supposedly stole from your father? What kind of daughter does that make you?"

She looked at him with a malicious glare. "I'm an excellent daughter. I *have* and always *will* obey my father's commands. I'm sorry, Matt. When it all boils down to it, if it's between you and him, I'll always choose him."

"Listen to yourself. 'Obey' your father's 'commands?' That sounds more like a dictatorship than a father-daughter relationship."

"Whatever. It works for us," she said nonchalantly.

"Look. I get that you respect your father. I wouldn't expect otherwise. But the point is, I want Amanda to be able to respect *her* father as much as you respect *your* dad. So, you and William can think whatever you want about me. I have faith in our justice system, and I'm innocent, so I'm not really worried about that. I just want to make sure that you aren't sharing your suspicions with Amanda. Just let it play out, and then Amanda can make her own decisions."

For a long moment, Shelia didn't respond. "I have to go," she said. "This has been fun."

Matt rolled his eyes. *Same crap. Different day. This conversation is going nowhere,* he thought. "Okay," he replied.

She grabbed her purse, and Matt followed her to the door. As she left, she paused on the front porch, turning around. "And Matt?"

"What?" he asked.

"I wouldn't count on that 'faith' you have in our justice system. In this county, my daddy is more powerful than you realize, and your number one on his shit list. I'm just saying. Thanks for the sex—and the breakfast."

With that, she turned around and sauntered toward her car.

***

The next day, Matt went to work feeling refreshed and relieved. The sheriff called and confirmed that he had passed the lie-detector test, so he was confident that the whole thing was a big misunderstanding. He was still bumfuzzled about the tryst with Shelia, but he resolved to be unyielding from now on. The fact that she even entertained the idea of him being a thief secured his decision. Their relationship was over—for good this time.

"Matt, there's a man out here looking for you," Tom said, interrupting Matt's thoughts.

"Cool," Matt replied. "Who is it?"

"He says his name is Daniel Manning."

"For real? That's an old buddy of mine," Matt said, beaming. "Tell him I'll be there in a second." Matt put his screwdriver down, dusted off his pants, and headed to the front of the shop. "Daniel," he yelled. "Man, it's good to see you. What brings you over here? You need a trailer?"

Daniel shifted his feet and stared at the ground. "Hey, Buddy. No, I don't need a trailer, but I need to talk to you. It's important."

The serious look on Daniel's face concerned Matt. *Now what?* "Okay, man. What's up?"

Seeing other workers close by, Daniel looked around and whispered, "Is there somewhere we can talk—more privately?"

"Yeah. Sure, man," Matt said. "Come on around back. I have a picnic table out here."

Daniel followed Matt and sat down at the table. He clasped his hands together and tapped his fingers nervously.

"What's going on, Daniel? You're kinda freaking me out."

"Look," Daniel said. "I know we haven't talked in a long time, but in the past, you were always a good friend to me, and I know what a good person you are."

"Of course," Matt said.

"Let me get right to it, then." Daniel paused. "I'm friends with Jake Gazaway. I don't know if you know him, but he's a sheriff deputy, and he's an alright dude, but he's loud and obnoxious—you know the type—the kind of guy who's always bragging and can't keep his damn mouth shut."

"Yeah, I don't know him," Matt said.

"Anyway," Daniel continued. "He came over for a barbecue this weekend, and he got to drinking a good bit, and well, he started talking about you."

"About me?" Matt asked. "I don't even know him."

"Yeah. Well, that's the thing. He was telling everybody that William thinks you paid some people to rob his house."

"Jesus. Not this again. I took a damn lie-detector test."

"Yeah, well, that's another thing. He mentioned that you took a lie-detector test, but then he was bragging about how the sheriff is a genius, saying that he told you that you passed, but that sheriff is spreading rumors around town that you failed—just to make you mad and see what you'll do next."

"What kind of crap is that?"

"I don't know, man. Sounds like some small-town Barney Fife shit to me, but I didn't want you to hear it from somebody that doesn't have your best interest at heart. I mean, I know you. I know you'd never rob anybody."

"I don't know what to do. This is ludicrous. I've done nothing wrong."

Daniel shifted in his seat. "I didn't even tell Jake that I knew you. I just ignored him and changed the subject, so I don't want you to think I was participating in this crap."

"Naw, man. I just—I just can't figure out where these accusations are coming from."

"Well, you know me. I'm just a good-ole-boy carpenter, and I ain't very savvy on the law or anything, but if you ask me, I'd get a lawyer."

Matt sighed and ran his fingers through his hair. "Honestly, I haven't even thought about talking to a lawyer. I mean, I didn't have anything to do with it, so there can't be any evidence against me."

"Yeah, well, it couldn't hurt just to talk to an attorney," Daniel said, reaching over and putting a hand on Matt's shoulder. "I'm sorry about all this, Man."

***

That afternoon, Matt's stomach churned as he drove to pick up Amanda from school. He hadn't spoken to Shelia since their wild rendezvous, and she didn't really agree to keep Amanda out of the situation with the robbery, so he didn't know what she may have told her.

"Surely, she wouldn't tell our daughter that I had something to do with this crap," he said aloud as he wiped sweat from his brow.

He had considered Daniel's advice but still hadn't consulted an attorney because, in his heart, he believed in the justice system—he was confident that he couldn't be implicated in a crime he didn't commit.

"Maybe I'm being naïve," he said, talking to himself again.

Matt's mind was still whirring when he pulled up to Amanda's school, but seeing her walk down the pathway eased his stress, and he smiled at her as she opened the truck door.

"Hey, Baby Girl," Matt said exuberantly. "How was school?"

Amanda crawled in and responded with downtrodden eyes. "Hey, Daddy. It was fine."

Matt removed his hand from the gearshift and physically turned his body toward his daughter. "Hey. Look at me. Something's wrong. I can tell by your voice. Tell Daddy what's wrong."

"Uh. Well, uh."

"It's okay. You can tell me," Matt said.

"Mama said you stole from Pop," she blurted out, tears streaming down her face. Then she reached into her pocket and pulled out a folded sheet of paper. She thrust it toward Matt. "Mama said to ask you these questions."

Matt was so astonished; he couldn't even say a word. He accepted the paper, and fury washed over him as he opened it and read the hand-written list.

1. Ask Daddy if he planned the whole break-in by himself.

2. How much money did Daddy get to keep from this deal?

3. Does Daddy have Pop and Nonna's jewelry?

4. What other illegal activity has Daddy been involved in?

5. How long has Daddy been planning this?

6. Why does Daddy hate Pop so much?

7. Did Daddy take us on vacation to make it look better for him?

> 8. Why did Daddy do this? Did he do it for the money? Or was he jealous of Pop?

As Matt read the list, he heard a car horn beep. He craned his neck around and saw the woman behind him in the pickup line giving him a dirty look.

"Just a minute," he yelled out his window. Then he turned to Amanda, who quietly whimpered. "Amanda. I didn't do this. You know me. I would never do something like this."

"But Mama said—"

"I don't care what your mama said!" Matt yelled. Then he took a deep breath and reached for Amanda's hand. "I'm sorry I yelled. Baby girl, I don't know why your mama is saying I did this, but I promise you. I had nothing to do with the robbery that happened while we were in Florida."

Amanda wiped her eyes on the sleeve of her jacket. The car behind them in line honked again—longer this time.

"Okay. We've got to go, but look at me, Baby. Look at me, please."

With wide, teary eyes, Amanda glanced up at Matt.

"This isn't true. Your daddy is not a thief. Have I ever lied to you?"

"Nooooo," she wailed.

"Okay," he said, patting her leg. "We'll figure this out. Everything's going to be okay. Let's go home."

Even as he said it, doubt entered his mind. *Maybe I do need an attorney,* he thought as he drove away.

***

When he pulled into his driveway, he shut off the engine and again turned to Amanda.

"Baby girl, I'm not even going to ask you what your mama told you about all this, but you have to understand something. None of this is your fault. You're a kid, and you shouldn't have to worry about adult problems. Your mama shouldn't have involved you. And no matter what she said about me, you won't ever hear me say anything bad about her. She's your mama, and you love her. And I know it's been tough with me and Mama splitting up, but Baby, you don't have to pick a side. You love us both, and that's okay. That's the way it should be."

Amanda wailed. "I just want things to go back to the way they used to be," she said through sobs.

"Oh honey," he said, stroking her hair. "Honestly, I do, too, but sometimes, we just can't have everything we want. The truth is, life isn't fair. And this won't be the only time that you're upset by things you can't control. The important thing is how you handle situations like this. You have to be strong—keep going—and know that things will look up, eventually."

"Okay," she said, still crying.

"And hey, you're the most amazing kid I know. You're kind and smart—and strong. I love you so much, and your Mama loves you, too. No matter what happens, we will always be there for you—both of us."

"Oh, Daddy, I love you too," Amanda said, reaching for Matt.

He embraced her in a hug, and he felt her sob against his shoulder. *I wish I could protect her from all the pain in the world,* Matt thought. *God, please just watch over her when I can't.*

"Okay," Matt said, pulling away. "Enough of this sappy stuff. You're at Daddy's house now, so that means its fun time. What do you say we bake some cookies?"

Amanda smiled and wiped away her tears. "I have homework, Dad, and we both know you can't bake."

Matt laughed, deep and loud. It felt good to sincerely smile—to laugh. "Okay, after homework, and I bought some of those pre-made cookies you put on a cookie sheet and bake. Surely, your ole Dad can't mess those up. Besides, that's why you're here—to make sure I don't burn the house down."

Chapter Six

Matt situated Amanda at the kitchen table with her homework, and he pre-heated the oven to bake the cookies. *Cookies before dinner?* he thought. *Oh well. She's had a horrible day. It won't hurt her.*

"How's that homework coming?" Matt asked.

"Almost done," Amanda said, her voice more upbeat now.

"Good deal. I'm pre-heating the oven, so when you're done, we'll bake the cookies. I gotta run to the bathroom. I'll be right back. Don't get into any trouble while I'm gone," Matt said with a wink.

Amanda rolled her eyes and said, "Don't fall in the toilet." Then she laughed so hard, she snorted.

"Was that a snort?" Matt asked with a chuckle.

"Yep," Amanda said.

In the bathroom, Matt closed the door and slid to the floor, sitting on the cold tile. He put his head in his hands and desperately tried to hold back tears.

I can't believe Shelia gave that paper to Amanda. That's ridiculous. Hell, that's child abuse.

Matt wanted to punch something—anything, but he refrained, knowing that Amanda was just yards away.

Shelia was my wife. She freaking knows me—she has to know that I wouldn't do something like this. It doesn't make sense. And why did she come over here yesterday? The whole thing is so bizarre. She had me record us having sex—and she asked me to hit her? Was she trying to set me up? To have a video of me being violent? Maybe this whole thing is her way of getting revenge because I wouldn't get back with her. If so, that's terrible. How could she do this to Amanda? I always knew she was selfish, but this takes it to the next level.

And what about William? What's his motive? I know he said that I embarrassed him by divorcing Shelia, but people get divorced all the time—and most fathers-in-law don't try to punish their ex-sons-in-law. Whatever's going on, I need to protect myself. I'll call an attorney tomorrow. If the Carsons are going to tarnish Amanda's mind like this, then she needs me.

Matt rose from the floor and walked over to the toilet. He flushed the commode for good measure so that Amanda would think he made an ordinary trip to the restroom. Then, he went over to the sink and splashed water on his face.

Okay. Game face, he thought, and he opened the door, yelling, "Is it cookie time?"

Just then, the doorbell rang. Amanda was putting a textbook in her backpack.

"I'll get it, Amanda. You done with your homework?"

"Yes, sir," she said.

"Awesome. Get the cookies out of the fridge and start putting them on the cookie sheet."

When Matt opened the door, his eyes sprang open wide. Five uniformed police officers stood on his porch.

"Mr. Grant?" a tall officer with black hair asked.

"Yes," Matt replied in a whisper.

"Can you please come out on the porch?"

"What's this about? I have my daughter here with me."

"I understand, but I need you to come outside."

Matt glanced back at Amanda and saw that she hadn't noticed the officers. Matt slipped through the open door onto the porch, closing the door behind him. As soon as the door shut, the officer who had been speaking to him grabbed Matt's writs and twisted them behind his back.

"Matt Grant, we're arresting you for conspiracy to commit a crime and for burglary of a dwelling. You have the right to remain silent. Anything you say can and will be used against you in a court of law. You have the right to an attorney. If you cannot afford an attorney, one will be appointed for you."

It all happened so fast.

His mind in a haze, Matt could barely process the officer's words, but the fog lifted when he saw the door open. Amanda stepped out onto the porch, and Matt yelled, "Amanda, go back into the house!"

"Daddy," Amanda screamed, and she ran to him, wrapping her arms around his waist.

"It's okay, Amanda. It's okay. It's all a misunderstanding. Remember what we talked about earlier? You have to be strong. Everything's going to be okay. Go back in the house."

"No, Daddy. No," Amanda sobbed.

Just then, Matt saw Shelia's car pull into his driveway. "What's Shelia doing here?" Matt asked aloud, to no one in particular. "Oh my, Lord. She *knew*. She knew they were going to arrest me, and she let me pick up Amanda anyway," he said to himself, with Amanda still gripping him.

"Okay, honey," an officer said, putting his hand on Amanda. "We have to go now. You have to let go."

"Don't touch my daughter," Matt said to the officer. With his hands behind his back, he kneeled so that he was eye-level with Amanda. Tears poured down her face. "Hey, Baby Girl. Look, your Mama's here. Go get in the car with Mama, and don't worry about me. The police just want to ask me some questions, but everything's going to be alright."

"No, Daddy. I want to stay with you," she cried.

"Oh, Amanda, those are the sweetest words I've ever heard, but you can't come with me right now. You have to go with your Mama, okay? Be strong, Baby Girl, and hey—I love you. I love you more than anything."

Amanda's sobs had turned into breathless bawls, but she nodded her head.

"Okay. Go to your Mama. Run, baby. Run."

Amanda turned and jetted down the driveway to Shelia's vehicle.

With his hands in cuffs, Matt couldn't wipe away the tears streaming down his face.

"Let's get this over with," he said to the officer to his left.

***

At the jail, when the police officer removed Matt from the car, reporters swarmed him.

"Did you rob your father-in-law?"

"Where's the money?"

"How much money did you steal?"

How in the heck did they know to be here waiting? Matt thought. Maybe he really *was* naïve. He had just come around to believing that the police were considering him as a suspect, but he had no idea that they would actually arrest him.

So, Shelia knew I was going to be arrested, and all these reporters knew, too. Seems like everyone knew but me.

Matt had seen enough crime procedural dramas to know how to handle reporters, so he put his head down and muttered, "No comment."

Inside the jail, Matt was surprised to only see uniformed officers. *Where are the other prisoners?* Matt thought. The officer who arrested him shoved Matt into a chair beside a desk and said, "Wait here."

After a few minutes passed, an older officer approached the desk and said, "Mr. Grant, I'm Jim Ray, and I'll be processing your booking. We've already run your record, so I know you've never been arrested before. Let me explain how this is going to work. First, I'm going to take down some information from you, and then we'll get your fingerprints. Then, we'll give you your prisoner clothes and have you change. After that, we'll take your mugshot and place you in your cell. Do you have any questions?"

"Um. Yeah. I didn't do this, so you can't have any evidence to prove that I did, so how were you able to arrest me in the first place?"

"Mr. Grant, we'll get into all that after we get your booking done. You'll have an opportunity to talk to the detective on the case."

"Okay. What about a phone call? Don't I get a phone call?"

"Yep. Again, that's after booking."

"Alright. But how come I'm the only non-police person here? You mean to tell me that I'm the only person who's been arrested today?"

"You'll have to take that up with Sheriff Tucker. I don't make the calls—I just take orders. Any other questions?" he asked.

"Yeah," Matt said. "Can you take these cuffs off?"

"Yes, sir," Officer Ray said. "We'll get them off as soon as I fill out this form."

Matt's stomach churned with anxiety as the officer typed on the computer.

What the hell did he mean when he said that I'd have to take it up with the sheriff? Sheriff Tucker—that's the man I spoke to when I came in and took the lie-

detector test. And when William's house was broken into, the sheriff called him personally. William said they were friends from way back. Surely, they couldn't just arrest me because William asked them to. That's not how the law works—or am I just being naïve again?

***

After booking, Matt sat in a cell alone and cold, isolated with only his thoughts to keep him company. He kept going over it in his mind. How could they arrest him? They couldn't have any evidence on him. It simply didn't make sense.

After an hour, a young officer walked up to Matt's cell and said, "Mr. Grant, I'm sorry to tell you that our phones are out of order, so you won't be able to make a phone call until we get them fixed, but I'm going to take you to an interrogation room so you can talk to the detective on your case."

Matt looked up and recognized the officer. "Rob? Rob Williams? Hey man. Remember me? We went to high school together."

"When I open your cell, please make sure you keep your hands to your sides. Then follow me."

"Rob. Hey, you know me. You know this is some bullshit. What's going on? Where are all the other prisoners? And why won't anyone answer my questions?"

Rob looked around to make sure that none of the other officers were paying attention to them. "Look," he whispered. "Sheriff Tucker cleared the jail out so you'd be the only person here, and he specifically told us all not to speak to you—told us we'd lose our jobs if we disobeyed his orders."

"What the crap? How is that even legal?" Matt asked.

"I don't know," Rob whispered, his head still spinning on lookout. "All us officers think it's fishy, but we need our jobs. I don't know what's really going on, but all I know is that Sheriff Tucker has had a few meetings with your father-in-law, and, well, William donates a lot of money to the sheriff's department. Everybody knows how close the sheriff is to William."

"Well, it sounds like I'm being set up. What the hell can I do, Rob? Do you know which lawyer in town is best for this kind of thing?"

Rob noticed another officer looking his way, and his whisper was quieter now, barely audible. "I'm sorry, Matt. I can't help you. I need this job. I can't afford to lose it. So please, just stop talking to me."

Matt sighed.

In a louder, normal tone of voice, Rob said, "Please follow me, Mr. Grant."

Chapter Seven

Matt sat in the interrogation room for what felt like hours until another young officer opened the door and smiled.

"Can I get you something?" the officer asked, and Matt looked at him strangely, wondering where the sudden hospitality was coming from.

Might as well take advantage of it, Matt thought. "I could use a cup of coffee," Matt said with a wry smile.

"Coming right up," the officer replied, and he left the room.

Sitting in the room alone again, Matt prepared mentally by making a list of what he already knew.

1. *William's house was broken into while I was in Florida.*
2. *When I gave a statement, the sheriff talked to me personally. Then, he asked me to take a lie-detector test.*
3. *The sheriff's office told me that I passed the test, but my friend said that the sheriff was telling other people I failed.*

4. Shelia and I called it quits for good because she refused to get professional help for our relationship. This obviously made her mad.
5. Shelia told our daughter that I was a part of this.
6. Shelia showed up minutes after I was arrested, so she must have known that I would be arrested.
7. When I arrived at the jail, the press was already there, so the police had to have told them that I would be arrested.
8. No other prisoners are in the jail, and I'm in a solitary confinement cell.
9. The other officers were instructed not to speak to me.
10. I haven't had a phone call because the phones are 'not working.'

Matt wrung his hands together and shook his head. *I smell a rat,* he thought. *From the little I know about police procedure, none of this is normal. I know I didn't do it, so it has to be a set-up.*

His thoughts were interrupted by the sound of the steel door being pushed open. Matt glanced up and saw

Sheriff Tucker enter with a cup of coffee in his right hand.

"Mr. Grant, it's good to see you again, but I'm sorry it's under these circumstances. I brought you the coffee you requested." He took the chair from the corner and slid it in front of the table where Matt sat. Then he sat directly across from Matt.

"Thanks for the coffee," Matt said, accepting the hot cup and sipping it.

"It's just black—didn't know if you take cream and sugar," the sheriff said with an eel-like smile.

"Black's fine," Matt replied.

"Alright," the sheriff said, putting his hands on the table. "Let's get to it, Matt."

"Okay," Matt said.

"I'm going to be honest with you here, Matt. We know that you somehow orchestrated this whole break-in. We're still filling in all the details, but if you tell us how you planned it and how it was all supposed to go down, then life will be a lot easier for you."

Matt shook his head. "I didn't orchestrate anything, so I can't tell you what happened. And what about my lie detector test? Didn't it prove that I'm innocent?"

The sheriff donned a big smile and emitted a soft chuckle. "The results were inconclusive. Is this really how you want to play it, Matt? Fine. Let's try something different. Tell me about your buddy Sorbo."

"Sorbo?" Matt asked. "I don't really talk to him much anymore. We were friends years back, but he mostly hangs out with William now."

"So, he's been to William's house?"

"Yeah, of course. He and William are big buddies," Matt said, taking another sip of coffee.

"You say that you and Sorbo hardly talk anymore, but we know he called you while you were in Florida."

"Well, then, you also know that I didn't answer the phone. It's probably been a year since I talked to that guy."

"You could've called him back on another phone—maybe the landline from the condo in Florida."

"I didn't," Matt said.

"Well, what about Daniel Greer and Justin Hinder? Tell me about your relationship with them."

"What?" Matt asked. "I know *of* those guys, just because we live in a small town, but I don't personally know either of them. They both have a pretty bad reputation, from what I've heard."

"Mmhmm," the sheriff responded, writing on a legal pad that Matt just noticed. "What else have you heard about them?"

"Well, honestly, I heard that my ex-wife slept with that Greer character."

"And that makes you angry, right?"

"Well, it doesn't make me happy," Matt said.

"So, a good way to get back at Shelia would be to ruin her father—that would be a good plan for revenge, I would think."

"Wait a minute. That's just ridiculous," Matt said, his voice rising.

"I'm just saying, it's common knowledge that you've always hated William, and..."

"Common knowledge? That isn't true, so how could it be common knowledge? Is this coming from William?"

"Again, I'll be honest with you. We *have* spoken to William, and he's adamant that *you* are the perpetrator of this crime."

"So that's it? You just arrest me because William said I did it? What's your evidence?"

"Honestly, Matt, William isn't just any ordinary citizen. He has a long history of supporting this department—of being an upstanding member of our community. As a witness, his credibility is unshakable."

"As a witness to what?" Matt yelled. "He was on vacation, just like I was when all this went down."

"Yeah, and you knew where he was going and how long he would be there."

"You know what? I know plenty about William Carson. An upstanding member of our community, my ass. He hangs out with thugs, and he deals with cash so he doesn't have to pay taxes, so don't act like you're following his orders because he's such a good person. You're minding him because he gives you money."

"Ahhh," the sheriff said, and he laughed loudly. "There it is. There's that hatred for William that I knew was there. And now you're accusing me of taking a bribe—of doing William's bidding for money? That's funny, seeing as William's life savings has suddenly up and vanished."

Matt crossed his hands over his chest and said, "I'm done with this. I'm not saying another word until I talk to an attorney."

Sheriff Tucker gave Matt a serious look. "I know you, Matt Grant. I know everyone in this community. And I know you think you're better than most of us—us *ignorant* rednecks. You don't drink. You don't smoke. You hardly cuss. You're a church-going fellow. That's all fine and good, and I'm sure it grants you favor with the good Lord, but you're going to learn to respect the people in this town—the people that matter."

"What's that supposed to mean?" Matt asked.

"It just means that I'm giving you a chance—a chance to make this easy on yourself, but if you want to fight us on this, then you have no idea what you're in for, Buddy."

"I'm not your buddy," Matt said coolly. "And like I said, I'm not saying another word until I talk to an attorney."

***

In solitary confinement, the days proceeded indistinctly, and Matt lost track of how much time had passed—or what day it was. With so much time alone, he had determined that William was the mastermind behind this set-up—and he feared the extent of William's co-conspirators in this frame-job, seeing as Shelia seemed to be a part of it too.

One day, an officer came to his cell and announced, "You have a visitor."

"Is it my mama?" Matt asked.

"Follow me, please," the officer replied, ignoring Matt's question.

"Ahhh, I see the command not to speak to me personally is still in order," Matt said, rising from the cold bench of his cell.

The officer led Matt to another interrogation room where a short, pudgy man sat at the table. He wore an expensive suit, Matt noticed, but he fidgeted nervously, and when Matt entered, he jumped up from the table as if he was startled.

"Mr. Grant," the man said. "Hi. I'm Jack Ford. I'm an attorney, and I'd like to talk to you about your case."

"Did my mama send you?" Matt asked, moving toward the table and sitting down.

"Well, uh," Ford stuttered. "Yeah. Well, I heard you needed a lawyer, so I'm here to see if I can offer you some assistance."

Matt was usually a good judge of character, so he appraised the attorney. His eyes were too close together, which gave him the appearance of a weasel. He continued to fiddle with papers, and he swirled the pen in his hand anxiously. As far as first impressions went, Matt wasn't impressed, and his gut told him that this wasn't a reliable man.

But if Mama sent him, he must be good, Matt told himself. *Hear him out.*

"Well, I do need an attorney," Matt said.

"Yes, yes, you do," Ford said. "I've reviewed the police report associated with your arrest, and honestly, it looks like they don't have much on you. With that being said, I'm confident that I can get these charges dismissed."

"Dismissed—as in all of this goes away?"

"Uh, yeah. Yeah. Exactly. It'll all go away. Now, all I need you to do is sign this agreement, and I'll need a retainer. You can have a family member pay that, or you can wait and pay me after you set bail. You should be seeing a judge tomorrow, and because you have no priors, getting you released on bail shouldn't be a problem," he said.

"How much is this going to cost me?" Matt asked.

The weasel-man smiled, and his strange eyes crinkled with delight. "Can you really put a price on your freedom?" he asked.

Once again, Matt felt his stomach perform a somersault.

***

The bail hearing was unimpressive. Officers ushered Matt across this street, where his weasel attorney spoke to Judge Barry Davis. The judge set a $500,000 bond, which sounded pretty high to Matt, considering he had never been arrested before, but the DA argued that Matt was well-off and presented a flight-risk. Matt was pretty ignorant regarding bail procedures, as he had no history with this sort of thing, so he asked his attorney if he'd have to pay 500 grand to get out.

In his jittery voice, Ford told Matt, "No, no. It's okay. We'll get a bail bondsman to deal with the bond. You don't have to pay the whole $500,000. You only pay ten percent. I'll contact your mother and get a bail bondsman to meet her down here," he said, and then, he skittered out of the courtroom.

When they escorted Matt back across the street, they took him to an interrogation room instead of placing him back in a cell. In minutes, Sheriff Tucker entered, followed by a tall, lean man with graying hair.

"Matt, this is detective Sam Robinson. We wanted to have a little talk with you before you made bail," Sheriff Tucker said.

Matt rolled his eyes. "Tucker, I've already told you that I'm not talking to you without my attorney present."

"Hang on there," Robinson said. "I just want to give you something to think about."

"What?" Matt asked sullenly.

The detective sat down in the chair across from Matt while the sheriff stood in the corner. "We arrested Sorbo, Greer, and Hinder, too, all in-connection with this burglary. But, just like you, they're making bail, too. They'll be released by tomorrow, at the latest."

"So?" Matt replied.

"So," the sheriff said from the corner, "you yourself said that they don't have the best reputations."

Detective Robinson continued. "Let's be honest. They're thugs—probably even dangerous. We've talked to all of them, and they *may* have the impression that you're throwing them under the bus—that *you're* the reason they were even arrested in the first place."

At this point, Matt wasn't even surprised. "And why would they think that?" Matt asked, his voice dripping with sarcasm.

"Well, your name may have come up during our discussions," Detective Robinson said, donning an artificial look of sympathy.

"I haven't thrown anyone under the bus. The only reason I knew they were involved at all was because *y'all* told me they were."

"Well, *I* know that, and *you* know that," Detective Robinson said. "But *they* don't know that. So, they might be inclined to want to shut you up."

"So, you're saying that my life might be in danger?" Matt asked.

Sheriff Tucker came over, dragging a chair. He sat down and donned a sinister smile. "Well, actually, Matt, your buddy Sorbo seems to be pretty afraid of you—he said you're quite the martial arts expert. And he said that he knows you hunt—so he knows you have some guns. But he did mention your daughter—said he's pretty familiar with her schedule since he hangs out with William so much."

Matt felt heat rise from his toes all the way to his cheeks, and his face reddened with anger. "He threatened my daughter, and you didn't do anything about it?" Matt asked through clenched teeth.

"Hey, hey, hey," Detective Robinson said. "We never said he threatened her, but we're trained to read between the lines. And he also mentioned your mother too—said she was elderly and not in good health. Are the two of you very close?"

Matt put his head in his hands, and though he tried to suppress the tears, they fell anyway.

"I know it's tough," Detective Robinson said. "But if you talk to us, we might be inclined to tell Sorbo and the other guys that you're not implicating them. We might even be able to have an officer watch your family—

to make sure they'll be okay. That's a perfectly acceptable response to you helping us with this investigation."

"But if you refuse to comply—decline to speak with us at all, well then, we have no reason to correct Sorbo's assumption—or to look out for your family," Sheriff Tucker added.

Matt looked up and angrily wiped the tears from his eyes. "This is blackmail, and you know it."

"I don't know anything, Matt," Sheriff Tucker said. "I'm just trying to conduct an investigation, and I'd appreciate your help."

"Okay," Matt said. "I'll talk to you. Of course, I'll talk to you if it means protecting Amanda and Mama. The two of them are the most important people in the world to me."

"Good boy," Sheriff Tucker said patronizingly.

"What do you want to know?" Matt asked.

Chapter Eight

After an excruciating ninety-minute interrogation, Matt felt worse than ever. They had grilled him about Sorbo—about how he knew him and about conversations they had months ago. It all happened so fast, it was a blur now. He closed his eyes and thought about what he had said.

"Didn't Sorbo tell you that you ought to steal all the money from your father-in-law's safe?" the detective had asked.

"Yeah. He said that one time, a long time ago, but a lot of William's friends have kidded around about stuff like that. You gotta understand. William brags about money all the time, and he pisses people off, so I've heard quite a few people talk about how they could even with him, but it's always just been talk. So, of course, when Sorbo said something similar, I just took it as a joke. Heck, one of William's friends even said he was going to set up a meeting with the IRS to get William busted for tax fraud," Matt told them.

"Are you trying to tell me that all of William's friends hate him? Does that include you?" the sheriff asked.

"No. I'm not saying that, and I don't hate William, but a lot of his 'so-called' friends don't really like him. He's screwed a lot of people over."

"Come on, Matt," Detective Robinson said. "You're a logical guy. They wouldn't be his friends if they didn't like him. If people were telling you stuff like that, then they were doing it because they knew you and William had some animosity."

"I really didn't think we had any animosity, though. I mean, yeah, he was my father-in-law, and we didn't always see eye-to-eye, but most people have a strained relationship with their in-laws, and for the most part, we got along."

Detective Robinson looked at Matt skeptically. "William says he's sure you did this, and Sorbo says it's true, too—that you planned the whole thing to get back at William."

Matt put his head in his hands, and tears formed in his eyes. "Look. I know Sorbo is a shady character. He's had some issues with drugs in the past, and who knows what all he's into. So, if he's saying I had a part in this, then he's just trying to set me up. Honestly, he'd probably do anything William told him to. Maybe William told him to say I did it. I don't know, but when he joked about robbing William, I told him that I didn't do stuff like that, and that was the truth. Stealing goes against everything I believe in."

"Sorbo knows about the safe and specific details about how much money was in it. You saying that William told him all that just to set you up? Sheriff Tucker asked.

"I don't know. Maybe Sorbo did it on his own. I already told you—Sorbo and William hang out all the time. At some point, I'm sure William told him about the safe and bragged about all the money he kept in there." Matt paused for a moment. "Crap. This *is* all my fault," Matt continued, distraught. "If I hadn't introduced Sorbo to William, this would've never happened."

Detective Robinson put his hand on Matt's shoulder. "It's okay. Let it all out. It's not your fault for introducing William to Sorbo, but you got greedy, didn't you? You wanted William to pay for being cruel to you. Hell, we know William. He's mean as a snake. I get it, and it was too easy—all you had to do was to get your thug friend to do the dirty work, and William wouldn't have anything else to brag about—he'd finally suffer like he's made you suffer over the years."

Matt shook his head. "No. No. I didn't have anything to do with this. Look, if Sorbo's getting out on bail, you can let me wear a wire. I know he'll talk to me, and I can get him to tell me the truth, whether William's just trying to set me up or if he did it all by himself."

Sheriff Tucker held up a hand. "No. We can't do that. You've already admitted that you and Sorbo talked about robbing William, so you committed conspiracy, and we can't implicate Sorbo solely after you've made that confession."

"Conspiracy? We didn't talk about robbing William. Sorbo made a joke."

"Joke or not, you admitted that the conversation took place."

"So, it's conspiracy even if it was a joke?" Matt asked incredulously.

"Yes. I'm afraid so," Detective Robinson said.

"Fine. If that's conspiracy, then I'm guilty," Matt said, "but I didn't rob anyone—and I don't plan on ever robbing someone. I just want my family to be safe."

Back in his cell, Matt worried about talking to them without his attorney, and even after the whole conversation, neither Sheriff Tucker nor Detective Robinson assured him that they'd put protection on his mom and daughter.

Stupid, stupid, stupid, Matt thought.

Just then, Rob Williams appeared. "Hey Matt. You've made bail."

"I did?" Matt asked. "How? Who did it? Can I leave?"

Rob looked around, seeing that no one else was paying attention to him. "I think your attorney set it all up. I don't know who made the bail, but Daniel Manning's out there to pick you up. I haven't seen him in years. Y'all still friends?"

Not in the mood to reminisce, Matt responded curtly. "Yeah. We are, and he's not under orders to ignore me."

Rob looked down. "I'm sorry, man. I really am. Anyway, follow me, and we'll get your bail processed."

***

That night, Matt stayed at Daniel's house, but sleep was infrequent and restless. The next morning, Matt walked into the kitchen, and Daniel was at the stove, frying bacon.

"Hey man," Daniel said. "Have a seat. You want some coffee?"

"Yes. I've never been much of a coffee drinker, but lately, I need the caffeine."

"Not sleeping much, huh?" Daniel asked.

"Afraid not," Matt replied as he sat down at the kitchen bar.

"How do you take your coffee?" Daniel asked.

"Black will be fine," Matt replied. "Look, Daniel. I really appreciate you coming to get me."

"It's all good, Buddy," Daniel said with a sympathetic smile.

"So, what did Mama say? Was she freaked out?"

"She was definitely surprised—and scared, too," Daniel said as he slid a cup of coffee over to Matt. "But you know your mama. She tried to act like she wasn't afraid, but I could see it in her eyes. And I get it. You've never been arrested before, and this... well, this is all just ludicrous if you ask me."

"You're telling me," Matt said. "I still can't believe they arrested me. They literally don't have any evidence, just William saying he thinks I did it and some drug addict saying I set it all up."

"Who's the addict?"

"Mark Sorbo. You remember him?"

"Oh, Lord. Yeah. I remember him. He was cracked out in high school."

"Yeah, well, William hangs out with him now, and he's obviously saying that I set it up—had him go over there and rob William."

"That's it? They arrested you for that? That's pretty scary that they can bring charges against you based on the claims of a crackhead."

"Yeah. The only good thing is that the lawyer said he could probably get the charges dismissed."

"Well, look. I don't want to freak you out any more than you already are, but I'm just trying to look out for you. Anyway, my uncle was arrested a few years back on a big burglary charge, so I'm somewhat familiar with how all this works. I don't know if you're aware—but they're probably going to freeze your bank accounts."

"What? Are you serious? How can they do that? I'm an innocent man. Besides, I have employees to pay—not to mention paying the lawyer."

"Yeah, I mean, you have a little while—I'm not sure how long, but they give you some time to take care of business. They didn't tell you any of this down at the station?"

Matt put his head in his hands. "They didn't tell me anything. No one would even talk to me. Rob said the sheriff told all the officers they'd get fired if they spoke to me. I didn't even get a phone call. So, I was lucky that lawyer showed up and contacted Mama."

"Wow," Daniel said. "This whole thing is crazy. Well, the other thing is, they may be watching you, just to see what you'll do while you're out on bail, so I was thinking that you could drive my suburban for a while. Plus, in this small town, everybody's already heard about all this crap, so if you borrow my vehicle, it may help you lay low."

Matt looked up from his coffee cup. "Really? That's amazing, Daniel. Why are you doing all this? I mean, you don't have to do all this for me. I just... I just can't tell you how much I appreciate it."

Daniel turned around and faced Matt again. "Look, Man. You've always been a stand-up guy. Even in high school, I remember you reaching out to the kids who didn't fit in—being nice to them when none of the rest of us were. And, like I said, my uncle went through something like this, so I know how devastating it can be. Plus, I know your mom isn't in good health, and with your divorce, well, you need someone on your side."

Tears sprung to Matt's eyes, as if the weight of reality finally fell onto his shoulders. "Thank you."

Daniel turned back to the stove, and the room was quiet, except for the sound of the bacon frying.

"Hey," Matt said. "How'd it turn out for your uncle?"

Daniel froze, and with his back still to Matt, he said. "Well, he's in prison—got twenty-five years."

"Jesus," Matt said.

"But he was guilty—guilty as sin. Totally different scenario."

"I hope you're right," Matt said.

***

Later that day, Matt went to the bank to withdraw money to pay his employees and get cash for his attorney.

Walking up to the teller's window, he recognized Tammy Jones, and he felt his hands get sweaty. She smiled sympathetically at him.

"Maaaaatt," she said in her sweet, southern drawl. "How're you doing, darling? I hear about your trouble."

He smiled sheepishly. "I'm alright, Mrs. Jones. I didn't do anything wrong, so I think it'll all work out."

"Well, I'll tell you one thing," she said, whispering now. "Even if you *did* do it, I wish you didn't get caught. That William Carson. He's a piece of work. Excuse my language, but he's an asshole."

Matt laughed a bit and said, "Yeah, he has his moments."

"I'm serious," Tammy said. "My husband was supposed to do some work for him, and William plum cursed him out for showing up late one day—he didn't care that I had a flat and needed Paul to come change my tire—didn't want hear it. He fired Paul, right there, right on the spot."

"I'm sorry to hear that," Matt said, giving her the same sympathetic smile, she had worn when he came in.

"Anyway, what can I do for you today?"

"I need to make a withdrawal."

"Okay," Tammy said, typing on the keyboard. "Let me pull up your account. From your checking?"

"Yes, Ma'am."

"And how much will you be withdrawing today?"

"Twenty-five thousand," Matt replied.

Tammy glanced at him. "Oh. Wow. Okay. Well, with that amount, I have to get approval from the bank manager. It's Jenny Goodman. You know her. Just wait right there, and let me get this approved for you. Okay, honey?"

"Thank you," Matt said, and he glanced around the bank. *I wonder how many other people have heard about my 'trouble,'* he thought.

Just then, he saw Sam Robinson enter the bank. The detective locked eyes with Matt, and then he walked out the door. *Jesus. Daniel was right,* Matt thought. *They are following me.*

After Matt's transaction was finished, he walked out the door toward Daniel's suburban, but Detective Robinson was standing in the parking lot.

"Hey, Matt," Detective Robinson said.

"Jesus. What now?" Matt asked.

"I just have a few more questions for you. Could you come back to the station and have a talk with me? The more information we can get, the easier it'll be to clear all this up."

Matt ran his hands through his hair. "Yeah. I guess so," Matt said. "But I've got to get work soon."

"Of course," Detective Robinson replied. "It won't take long. I promise."

***

At the station, Matt waited in Detective Robinson's office.

At least I'm not in an interrogation room this time.

Detective Robinson entered and said, "Thanks for coming in, Matt." He smiled, and then he asked, "So I have a question for you. How're you going to live in Fulton after this?"

"What do you mean?" Matt asked.

"Well, I just mean, it's a small town. It hasn't even been a week, and now, everybody knows you robbed your ex-father-in-law."

Matt stood up. "I didn't rob anyone. I shouldn't have come here."

"Matt, please. Sit down."

Matt looked at him skeptically and sat back down in the chair.

"My patrol officer told me you stayed at Daniel's last night," Detective Robinson said.

"So that means you've been following me?" Matt asked.

"Only for your protection, Matt. We talked about that situation."

"If you say so," Matt said.

"Well, don't you think it's a little selfish to put your buddy in danger? He has a daughter, and now you've exposed them to the risk, too."

"You just said you had someone protecting me!" Matt said incredulously.

"Well, I..."

Just then, Sheriff Tucker walked in. "Good morning, gentlemen."

Matt rolled his eyes.

"Hey, Sheriff Tucker," Detective Robinson said. "I was just telling Matt here that we were looking out for him. As a matter of fact, I was making sure that no one was following him this morning. That's when we ran into each other at the bank. It looked like he was making a withdrawal."

"A withdrawal?" Sheriff Tucker asked. "How much did you withdraw, Matt?"

"I don't see how that's any of your business, sir," Matt replied.

"Well, why withdraw it? You planning on going somewhere?" Sheriff Tucker asked. "Do we need to talk to the judge? Amend your bail because you're a bigger flight risk than we thought?"

"Like I said, not that it's any of your business, but I needed the money to pay my employees and my vendors," Matt said.

"Well, I don't know why you couldn't write a check for that," Detective Robinson said. "That's what most legitimate business owners do. Seems to me, if you're dealing with cash like that, then you're involved in some nefarious business practices—perhaps matters of which we should be aware."

Matt stood up again. "I'm leaving. You said you had some questions about the case—questions that would bring out the truth of what really happened. And by the way, the truth is that I had nothing to do with any of this crap. But you just brought me in here to harass me, and I don't have time for this."

"Matt, wait," Sheriff Tucker said.

Matt ignored him and walked out the door.

Chapter Nine

On his way to work, Matt got a phone call from his friend Donnie.

"Hey, Donnie. How's the shingles business doing?"

"Oh, they're great, man."

"Good. Look, I haven't had a chance to call Nathan, but I'm still interested in y'all building a shop for me," Matt said. "I guess we need to work out a price."

"That's fine. I heard you've got a lot going on lately. Nathan said he'd handle the price and the contract. I'll tell him to get up with you. How're you doing?"

"I've Been better," Matt said.

"So I heard. Actually, that's why I'm calling," Donnie said.

"Thanks for calling. I think it's just a big misunderstanding. I didn't do anything wrong, so it'll all work out."

"Well, I wanted to..."

"Listen, Donnie, I really appreciate you calling, but my attorney told me not to talk to anyone about the case, and I know it's going to be hard since everybody in town is talking about it, but..."

"Hey. Let me interrupt you, Matt. I'm not calling to get the scoop or anything. I'm calling to give *you* some information."

"Oh. Okay," Matt said. "What's up?"

"Shelia called me."

"Why?" Matt asked.

"I don't know, man. She must be calling all your friends. Anyway, she told me that you already confessed to being the mastermind behind the robbery. So, I thought, damn, if she called me and told me this, then she's probably telling everybody that."

"Just for the record, Donnie, that's a damn lie. I didn't confess to anything because I didn't do anything."

"That's what I told her—that I didn't see you as the kind of person that would do something like this, but she was just like, 'I guess you never really know a person.'"

"Well, thanks for the heads up," Matt said. "At this point, nothing really surprises me anymore."

"But Matt... that's not it. There's something else."

"What?"

"Well, she also said that she heard you were trying to have her daddy murdered—that you were going to pay somebody to kill him."

Matt was so surprised; he almost ran off the road. "Was she serious?" he asked.

"Yeah. As far as I know. She wasn't joking—she said it all serious. Said she was warning me because we hang out. I mean, I told her that you wouldn't hurt a fly, and she said that her information came from a good source. Anyway, I can't imagine someone spreading shit like that about me, so I just wanted to let you know."

Tears flooded Matt's eyes again, and he held back a stifle. "Hey, Man. I appreciate it. I really do, and I'd like to think that I don't have to say it, but none of that's true."

"You don't have to tell me that. I know, Matt. I know this whole thing is daunting, but you've got a lot of support in this town. I know William thinks he runs things, but you're a good dude, and most people know that."

"Again, I appreciate it, Man."

When Matt hung up the phone, he couldn't stifle his grief anymore, and when he broke out in sobs, he slowed down because it was difficult to see through the tears.

***

At work, Matt pulled it together and tried to remain stoic for his employees. He explained the situation, telling them that he was innocent and that he was confident that all charges would be dropped. The rest of the day, he went through the motions robotically, still numb from the information that Donnie gave him.

After work, he was supposed to meet his mom at his cousin's house, and there, he would face his family for the first time since he was arrested. When he pulled into the driveway, he turned off his truck and closed his eyes. *Oh God. Please give me the willpower to be strong for Mama.* His stomach rumbled, and he realized he hadn't had lunch.

On the porch, as he knocked on the door, he said, "Knock-knock. It's Matt," and he opened the door and entered through the kitchen.

His mom, his aunt, and his cousin were sitting at the kitchen table, and as soon as his eyes locked onto his mother, tears formed in her eyes. She gently stood, and he walked toward her with his arms out.

When they embraced, he wanted to let it all go—to bawl like a baby—to crawl into her lap and hear her tell him that it'd all be okay. But he suppressed it all when he heard her crying gently into his shoulder.

"It's okay, Mama. It's okay. I'm alright."

She pulled away and wiped her eyes with a tissue from her pocket. "What in the world is going on, Matt? How did this happen?"

"Sit down, Mama," Matt said. "I'll explain it all to you. Just sit down and relax."

Just then, his Aunt Valerie came over and embraced Matt. "Hey, darling. It's good to see you. I just wish it was under better circumstances."

He hugged her back and said, "Me too, Aunt Val."

"Let me make you a plate," she said as she pulled away.

"I haven't had much of an appetite, but I know I need to eat something," Matt replied. "Thank you." Matt sat down at the table across from his mama. "Hey, Shea," he said to his cousin.

"Hey, Matt," Shea said sympathetically. "We're all here for you."

"Thanks," Matt said. "Okay. Where do I start?"

Matt told them everything, and when he finished, they remained silent for a long time, with their hands covering their mouths in astonishment.

"You're being set up," Shea said. "I wasn't even going to tell you this, but after hearing your story, I'm sure of it. The day you were arrested, they had it on the news that night. They had William on there, and he said that you planned it all—had some people break into his safe while he was on vacation. And he said that you took *his* daughter and granddaughter out of state for an alibi."

Matt shook his head.

"I don't know much about police procedure or anything," Shea said, "but I'm pretty confident that the proper protocol is not to allow someone to blab the whole case to the public like that before there's even a proper investigation. To be honest, I've never seen anything like it."

"Yeah," Aunt Val said. "It sounds like they'd already made up their minds about what happened the day they arrested you."

"Do you think William really believes you did it? Shea asked. "Or is it more nefarious than that? Surely, he wouldn't be trying to set you up, knowing you're innocent."

"I don't know anymore," Matt replied. "I mean, William's done some dirt—he deals with cash, doesn't pay his taxes, and he's been known to pop pills and drink a good bit. But, until all this went down, I never really considered him to be an evil person. But now, I don't know. I mean, I was married to his daughter, so he knows me. I'm the father of his granddaughter. So, it's not like I'm a stranger to him. He knows I've got good morals. Heck, that's one of the problems he had with me—he's called me a goody-two-shoes. So, as bad as it sounds, I really think he's setting me up, knowing I'm innocent."

"Oh Jesus," Matt's mama said. "Oh Jesus, please take care of my baby. Please protect him."

***

Matt hadn't seen Amanda since he was arrested, but she had a softball game every Tuesday during the summer, and until Matt was arrested, he had never missed a game, so he and his mother decided to attend.

At the ballpark, Matt helped his mama out of the truck, and as they walked to the ballfield, Matt could feel the stares on him, and he felt shame—not for doing anything wrong, but for having to put his mother through so much scrutiny, when she just wanted to see her grandchild.

Just as they made it to the field, Amanda appeared from seemingly nowhere, nearly knocking Matt down as she ran to him so hard.

"Daddy," she yelled. "You came."

He kneeled down and hugged her. "Of course, I came," he said.

"Well, I thought you might miss it, especially after those policemen put those handcuffs on you. And Mama said you're going to jail for a long time."

"Hey. You don't worry about me. I'm going to be okay. You just worry about whooping the eagles today."

"Can I come home with you after the game?" Amanda pleaded.

Matt glanced at his mother, and she had tears in her eyes once again. "I think you're going to have to stay with your mama tonight, baby girl. Daddy's working hard to get this misunderstanding all worked out, okay? But as soon as everything's cleared up, we're going to go on another trip, just you and me."

"Yay," Amanda squealed.

"Alright. Go over there and give MawMaw a hug," Matt said.

Tears streamed down his mom's face as she hugged her granddaughter. Matt took a deep breath and suppressed the threat of his own tears. He seemed to be doing that an awful lot lately.

Amanda's team won the game, and Matt kept his eyes on her the whole game. She seemed to be happy, playing and laughing with her friends, but he couldn't help but wonder how this would affect her. Adults were loose-lipped, and all the parents knew about his situation, so the kids probably knew too. If only he could protect her.

***

The next day, at work, Nathan Newton came to the shop. Matt had asked Nathan and Donnie to build him a shop before the whole break-in debacle. They worked together, so the plan was for Nathan to build the shop and for Donnie to install the singles for the roof. Matt knew Nathan through William, but Nathan had done work for him in the past, and his work was always excellent, but now, Matt wondered if he should find another worker.

"Hey, Nathan," Matt said. "I talked to Donnie this week. He said you'd give a price quote for the shop and draw up a contract. We can ride out there, and I'll show you the details."

Nathan looked nervous. "No. I mean, yeah. I'm still interested in the shop. Donnie told me to call you about it, but I, uh… that's not why I'm here. Is there somewhere we can talk?"

Here we go again, Matt thought. Matt took him to the picnic table behind the shop. "What's this all about?" Matt asked him.

"Well, my buddy, Tim Ware wants to talk to you," Nathan said.

"Tim Ware? Isn't he one of William's friends?"

"Yeah. They know each other," Nathan said.

"What's he want to talk to me about?" Matt asked.

"He knows what really happened with the robbery, says he wants to tell you, to help you out."

Matt shook his head. "If he knows all about it, then why doesn't he just tell the police? Or heck, he can tell my attorney. I don't know why he wants to talk to me."

"I don't know, Man. He just wants to talk to you, and since you don't know him, he asked me to set up a meeting. Will you meet with him or not?"

Matt blew out a breath. "My shop's open to the public. If he wants to come by, then nothing's stopping him."

Nathan nodded and started to walk back to his truck.

"Oh, and Nathan?" Matt said.

Nathan turned back around. "You can also tell him that I'll listen to what he has to say, but I ain't saying nothing. My attorney advised me to not talk about the case, and considering this Ware guy hangs out with William, then I oughta heed his advice."

An hour later, a big black truck pulled up to Matt's shop. Nathan got out of the passenger seat, and a small-framed man in his 60s got out of the driver's seat. The man wore thick glasses, and his face was pocked.

Matt approached them. "Nathan," Matt said.

"Matt, this is Tim Ware," Nathan said, nodding at Tim.

"Nice to meet you," Matt said, reaching his hand out to shake.

Tim shook his hand, but his grip was flimsy, his hand sweaty.

"I'm pissed at that mother-fucker Carson," Tim said, getting right to it in a high-pitched voice. His vulgar speech surprised Matt, but he remained silent. "That asshole's trying to pin this shit on me," he squeaked.

"On you?" Matt asked.

"Yeah. That's what I heard on the street—that William gave the cops my name, so I called that fucker and told him to meet me at a church parking lot, and when he did, I told him to leave me outta this shit, or I'd have him killed. I bet you feel the same way about that bastard. Don't you?"

"I don't want anyone to die," Matt said calmly. "And I know nothing about your involvement. Haven't heard your name come up at all."

"That piece of shit, Carson. I want that fucker dead," Tim said, and as he spoke, he flung his hands up in the air.

Matt glanced at Nathan. *This dude is on drugs,* he thought. *Why in the heck did Nathan bring this guy over here?*

"Nathan said you have some information about the case you wanted to share with me," Matt said.

"Yeah. I done told you. That fucker, William, says I was with Sorbo and we stole his goddamn money—said you told us to do it—that you'd give us a cut of the money—the shitbag."

"But I don't even know you," Matt said.

"That's what I'm trying to tell you," Tim yelled. "That fucker's trying to fuck us both up!"

Matt looked around the parking lot, noticing that clients and his employees were starting to stare.

"I... uh..." Matt started to say.

"Carson—that shitbag is evil. That's why we gotta end this fucking shit. Get rid of him somehow."

Matt straightened his cap. "Well, I appreciate the information, but I need to get back to work."

Tim jerked his head up and down and scowled. "Ain't you listening to me, you fucking asshole? William's trying to put us away. I'm trying to help your stupid ass. If we kill him, there ain't nobody pulling the strings, and all this shit'll go away."

"Like I said, I've gotta get back to work," Matt said. He glanced at Nathan, who was staring at his shoes. "It was nice to meet you, Tim. Nathan, you and Donnie still going to do that work for me, right?"

Nathan nodded.

"Alright. Good. Call me when you want to meet me at the shop," Matt said.

As he walked away, Matt heard Tim say, "That stupid motherfucker didn't go for it."

***

The next day, Matt's head was still reeling from Shelia's gossip and the bizarre meeting with Tim Ware, but he tried to focus on things he could control, so he called and set up a meeting with Donnie and Nathan about the new shop. Donnie and Nathan were already building Matt's new house—the house he originally thought he'd share with Shelia and Amanda. It would be lonely being in that big old house alone, but their work was impeccable, so he wanted them to build him an accompanying shop—even if he did meet Nathan through William.

At the home site, Donnie was all smiles, but Nathan acted nervous again. Matt just figured he felt awkward considering their mutual connection to William—or maybe he was embarrassed about that crazy meeting with Ware.

"What the hell was up with that dude you brought to my shop yesterday?" Matt asked Nathan.

"Uh. Well, I dunno. I didn't know what he had to tell you. I thought he might've known something that uh could uh help you out."

"Well, he was strung out on something, and the way he was talking, I'd be careful around him if I were you."

"Yeah, well... uh... I don't really know him that well," Nathan said.

"Whatever. It's fine," Matt replied. "Anyway, let's talk about the shop."

"Yeah. I, uh, I can't pour the concrete, but Donnie said he could do that part, along with the roof," Nathan said.

"Yeah," Donnie said. "So, here's how we'll do it. We're going to give you a total price for the shed, which will include the pricing for the roof and the concrete. You can give the whole amount to Nathan, and he'll just pay me for my work on the shingles and concrete instead of you paying us separately. Is that cool?" Donnie asked Matt.

"However y'all want to do it," Matt said with a smile.

"Okay. Well, we talked about it, and um... How does eighteen grand sound?" Nathan asked.

"That's for everything? The shingles, too?"

Donnie nodded. "Yeah. I'm giving you a wholesale cost on the materials."

"That's a really good deal. Thanks, y'all. Eighteen-thousand it is," Matt replied. "When do I pay you?"

"I, uh, well, I'll make up a contract, and then I can bring it by your shop tomorrow. You can pay after you sign the contract. You paying cash?" Nathan asked.

"Yep. I've already withdrawn money to take care of odds and ends, so that sounds good. Come by tomorrow, and I'll get y'all taken care of," Matt said.

Donnie smiled and stuck out his hand for Matt to shake. "Always good to see you, Matt. Again, I'm sorry for the unfortunate events you're dealing with right now."

Matt shook Donnie's hand. "I appreciate it. It'll all work out." Then Matt looked at Nathan. "Thanks, Nathan. I'll see you tomorrow."

Nathan stared at the ground and replied in a barely audible voice, "See you tomorrow."

***

The next day, Matt went to work again, and though he was still anxious, he was trying to regain some semblance of normal by sticking to his regular schedule. Immersing himself in work helped keep his mind off his problems—the betrayal of people he thought he could trust. The morning flew by, and before he knew it, his stomach was growling. Glancing at his watch, he saw that it was nearly 2 p.m., so he took a break to eat the sandwich he had packed that morning.

Matt sat at the picnic table behind his shop, and he looked around at all the brilliant colors of the leaves. The Autumn weather had delivered a bright sun, but the air was cool and crisp. *It's really beautiful out here,* Matt thought, and he closed his eyes, breathing in the fresh air. For a moment, he imagined that everything was back to normal. He'd pick up Amanda from school, and when he got home, he and Shelia would start dinner and help Amanda with her homework. Still immersed in the fantasy, one of his employees shocked him out of the daze.

"Hey, Matt. Sorry to interrupt your lunch. Nathan's here to see you," Adam said.

Matt opened his eyes and smiled. "No worries. I'm done eating. Hey, it's such a nice day today. Can you bring him back here? I have to sign a contract, so we can do it here at the table."

"Yeah, sure," Adam said.

As Nathan approached, Matt noticed how he stared at the grass, and his right hand twitched as he swung his arms. *What is the deal with him lately?* Matt thought. *Maybe he's doing some drugs like his buddy Tim.*

"Hey, Nathan," Matt said as he came closer. "Have a seat. You got the contract?"

"I got it," Nathan replied in a hushed voice.

"Are you okay?" Matt asked.

"Yeah. I'm fine. Why? Have you heard something?"

Matt gave him a weary glance. "Nope. Haven't heard anything. You're just not acting like yourself, and well, you brought that crazy dude up here the other day. I've still been thinking about it. What was up with that? He, for real, acted like he was all geeked out on something."

Nathan placed the contract on the picnic table and wrung his hands together nervously. "Yeah. Well, like I said, I didn't know what he wanted to tell you, and I don't know him that well. I've only met him a few times, but I think Tim's just a little high-strung. He's alright, though."

"I don't know about that. He might've been strung out, but he was still talking about murder, so based on first impressions, I wouldn't call him alright."

"I dunno. He just said he wanted to talk to you, so I... uh... well..."

"It's fine. Don't worry about it," Matt said, seeing that he had made him uncomfortable. "Alright. Let's do this. This the contract?" Matt asked, picking it up and reading it.

"Yeah."

"Looks pretty standard to me," Matt said, pulling out his pen.

"Yeah. Donnie said it's pretty much the same as the one you signed for the house," Nathan said.

Matt signed the contract and pulled out his wallet. He removed the money and handed it to Nathan. "Alright, so we're all good? You'll take care of Donnie?"

"Uh, yeah. I'll uh... yeah... and... uh... we'll get started next week if the weather's good."

"Good deal," Matt said.

Nathan stood and put the money in his wallet, but then he sat back down. Matt expected him to say something else, but he sat there silently, staring at his hands.

"You sure you're okay?" Matt asked.

"Yeah. I... uh... I just wanted to say... uh... I'm really sorry about the deal with William," Nathan said.

Matt ran his hands through his hair. "Yeah. It's a crazy situation. William and I have never been best buddies or anything, but I'm astonished that he thinks I'm involved with all this mess—and Shelia, too. I've always tried to do the right thing—to be honorable and to treat people the way I want to be treated, and I just feel like the world is turning on me... like everyone I ever trusted..." Matt's voice trailed off as he stared at the clouds in the sky, lost in thought.

"Yeah," Nathan said, breaking Matt's train of thought. "I... uh... I'm sorry."

Matt shook his head. "Anyway, sorry. I went off on a tangent there. Yeah. I think it'll all work out. William's a logical guy. When he sees that the evidence doesn't point to me, he'll probably focus his attention on trying to find the real perpetrator."

Nathan stood then, abruptly. "Alright. I... uh... I gotta go. Thanks for the payment."

Before Matt could even reply, Nathan had sprinted out of hearing-range.

So strange, Matt thought. *I feel like I'm living in the freaking twilight zone.*

Chapter Ten

The next week, Matt almost felt like things were getting back to normal. His lawyer had advised him not to speak to Shelia, but she hadn't reached out to him anyway, even when he talked to Amanda on the phone. At work, business was good, and even though people gave him sideways stares everywhere he went, he felt much better since his attorney seemed positive that the district attorney would eventually drop the case due to lack of evidence.

Matt left work early on Thursday afternoon. The October day was cool and inviting, so Matt stopped by the grocery store and bought himself a steak to grill. At home, Matt changed clothes and prepared the grill in his back yard. While the coals were getting hot, Matt sat in his patio chair with his feet up. He inhaled the cool, fresh air and the scent of burning coals. Birds chirped, and he heard the squealing of playing children in the distance. *Must be the neighbors,* he thought. Then he smiled, thinking about Amanda. When she was younger, she ran in the grass for hours, chasing Matt through the yard, yelling, "Tag. You're it." He could see it now—Shelia sitting on the patio, sipping a cosmopolitan, while Matt and Amanda played. He sighed. At one time, they were happy—all of them, and at the time, he had the gall to believe that it would last forever.

Suddenly, Matt saw movement in his peripheral vision. When he swung his head around to investigate, he came face-to-face with a revolver.

"What the heck is going on?" Matt asked, standing up.

"Put your hands up," an officer shouted.

Suddenly, five more officers appeared, all pointing guns at Matt.

Astonished, Matt put his hands in the air and said, "I don't know what's going on. Maybe y'all have the wrong house?"

The officer closest to him asked, "Are you Matt Grant?"

"Yes," Matt replied.

Then, in a blur, the officer moved to Matt, put handcuffs on him, and put him under arrest. Matt was so shocked, he barely responded, but then, as they walked toward a police car, his mind cleared.

"What's the charge?" Matt asked. "What are you arresting me for?"

The officer looked at him smugly. "Conspiracy to commit murder," he said.

Matt's heart dropped deep down into his stomach.

***

Back in an interrogation room at the jail, Matt was past the point of being angry. He was downright furious. He was an innocent man, and now, he'd been arrested twice, and this time, as he sat in the interrogation room, the cop had not removed his handcuffs. As the handcuffs dug deeper into his wrist, Matt's anger swelled.

Finally, Sheriff Tucker entered the room, smiling.

You sonofabitch, Matt thought, seeing his grin. "Conspiracy to commit murder? What the hell are y'all doing? I demand to see my lawyer. Who in the hell did I try to murder?"

Sheriff Tucker pulled up a chair, sat down, and smiled again. "We'll get your lawyer down here, but there's nothing he can do. Can't get bail again, so I guess you'll hafta be our guest until your trial."

Tears sprung to Matt's eyes, and he growled, frustrated at himself for showing the sheriff weakness. "You didn't answer me. Who did I supposedly try to murder?"

Sheriff Tucker chuckled, a deep belly laugh. "Oh, come on now, Matt. We have it all on tape. You gave Nathan Newton cash, and when Nathan met with Tim Ware to arrange the murder of your beloved ex-father-in-law, Nathan wore a wire. So, we have the whole transaction recorded."

He smiled again. "You going to tell me you didn't give Nathan a load of cash?"

Matt shook his head repeatedly. "No. No. No. This can't be happening. The money I gave Nathan was for him and Donnie to build my shop. We signed a freaking contract."

"You happen to have a copy of that contract on you?" Sheriff Tucker asked.

Matt growled again. "Yeah. It's at my shop at work. I don't keep it on me."

"Mmmm Hmmm," Sheriff Tucker said. "I'm sure you can get your lawyer to retrieve it for you. I just came in here to let you know what we have. We actually don't need any additional information from you. We've got all we need. Your employees verified that you had a meeting with Tim Ware earlier this week, and like I said, we have the cash exchange on tape."

"Tim Ware asked to meet with me!" Matt yelled. "I don't even know that guy, and he was strung out on something, not making any sense. I didn't ask him to do anything. He was saying that *he* wanted to kill William. I didn't say anything."

"Whatever you say, Matt," Sheriff Tucker said. "I'll have an officer escort you back to your cell. That'll be your new home for a while. I sure do hope our accommodations are up to your highfalutin standards."

With that, Sheriff Tucker stood and walked out the door.

***

In jail, Matt had no concept of time. He remained in a solitary cell, and none of the officers would speak to him to answer any questions. Again, he never received the opportunity to make a phone call because the phones were still 'out of order.' After what seemed to be weeks, his lawyer showed up, and an officer escorted him to what looked like a private conference room.

"Where the hell have you been, and what the heck is going on?" Matt asked his attorney.

"I've been investigating these charges. They're totally bogus. You've got nothing to worry about."

"Yeah, but I'm still in jail," Matt yelled.

"Well, you're going to a bond revocation hearing. I'm going to try to get you a new bond," Ford said.

"The sheriff said I couldn't get a new bond," Matt said.

"Well, I'm not going to lie to you. We probably won't be able to get you one, not with these charges."

"You just said they're bogus."

"Well, they are. The attempted murder charge won't stick, but considering the weight of the accusation, the judge probably won't reissue bail."

"This is total bullshit," Matt said. "Nathan set me up. He brought that drug addict to see me, and the money I gave Nathan was for him and Donnie to work on my new shop. That's it. I told the sheriff that I signed a contract."

Jack Ford peered at Matt and shook his head. "Yeah. The sheriff told me about the contract. I got it. I went to your shop and got it, so I'll enter that into evidence, and the charges will be dropped, eventually."

"What do you mean eventually?"

Ford was silent for a minute. "First of all, I believe you," he finally said. "But from the get-go, it doesn't look good. This Ware character comes to see you, and then he accepts a handful of *your* cash... from this Nathan guy. Anyway, like I said, it's all circumstantial, so it won't stick, but I doubt the judge will give you a new bond."

"So that means I'm staying here—in jail?"

"Probably. But I'll see what I can do. When we get to court, don't say a word. Let me do all the talking."

Matt nodded his head, but words failed him.

When they walked into the courtroom, the room was packed. After Matt sat down at the table, he whispered to Ford, "Who are all these people?"

"Attorneys. Spectators. Press. There's a lot of political pressure regarding this case. Your father-in-law obviously knows some important people." Ford nodded at the adjoining table. "That's the DA himself. He usually sends an associate to handle these hearings, but he's here in person today."

Eventually, the judge came in, and the crowd grew quiet. The judge had white hair, tan skin, and kind eyes. "Okay. Let's get this going," the judge said in an exasperated-sounding voice. "This is a bond revocation hearing for one Matt Grant. Mr. Simmons, I'm pleasantly surprised to see you here today representing the state."

"Thank you, sir," the district attorney said.

"Okay. Let's see what you got. It looks like the accusation is that Mr. Grant violated bond by committing an additional crime—conspiracy to commit murder?"

"Yes, sir. That is correct," Mr. Simmons said. "As you can see in our motion to revoke, we have evidence that Mr. Grant hired Mr. Tim Ware to murder Mr. William Carson. There was another man involved, Nathan Newton. He arranged the set-up, accepting the money from Mr. Grant and giving it to Mr. Ware."

"In the motion, it says you have a tape?" the judge asked.

"We do."

"Play the tape, then," the judge ordered.

The crowd stirred, and Matt tensed up as the court assistant prepared the tape. When the tape started playing, Matt felt fury mounting in his chest as Nathan's voice rang out in the courtroom.

"Okay," Nathan said. "Matt, um... instructed me to um... give you eighteen thousand in cash, just um... like you discussed."

"Fuck yeah," Tim said. "The fucking plan still the same? Kill that motherfucker Carson, right?"

"Um... yes... Matt wants you to, um... kill his father-in-law. That's um... what the money's for."

Matt wasn't surprised that Nathan sounded nervous on the tape. *Setting someone up for murder? Yeah, I'd be nervous too,* Matt thought.

"Okay. Done. That's fucking it, right?" Ware asked.

"Yeah. Uh. Does um... Joe know you're doing this?" Nathan asked.

"Fucking Joe Timmons? Fuck yeah. He knows."

"Well... um... if I um... get in trouble for all this... will um... do you think he could um... help me too?" Nathan asked.

"Fuck yeah," Ware said.

The tape ended, and the judge shook his head and glared at the DA. "That's pretty shaky evidence, Mr. Simmons. And why would these two be mentioning Joe Timmons? I'm assuming they're talking about Joe Timmons, the lawyer, since I'm not aware of any other 'Joe Timmons' in this county. With that being said, I don't know why an attorney would be aware of a murder-for-hire plot before it actually happens."

"I'm not sure why they mention Timmons," the district attorney replied. "I assume that Timmons may be representing Ware on another charge unrelated to this case."

The judge looked at the DA and shook his head. "I'm not convinced that Mr. Grant violated his bond, but I need to see the evidence for the original charge again before I make a decision. Are you prepared to show me that?"

"Yes, sir," the DA said. "We have a confession for the original charge."

"A confession?" the judge asked.

"I object," Ford said. "My client has confessed to nothing,"

The judge put his hands up. "Mr. Simmons, do you have a signed waiver of rights with the confession?"

"We do."

Ford whispered to Matt, "Did you sign a waiver of rights?"

"I didn't sign anything," Matt whispered back.

"I object," Ford said. "My client didn't sign a waiver of rights."

The judge chuckled. "You mean to tell me that someone forged his signature?"

"Perhaps," Ford said. "I haven't seen the document."

"Okay. Well, let's see if the confession is worth anything in the first place, and then we'll come back to the waiver. Mr. Simmons, I assume you have a tape of the confession."

"We do," Mr. Simmons said. "However, the tape is nearly an hour and a half long, sir. Therefore, I request permission to play the small portion in which Mr. Grant confesses."

"Objection," Ford said. "With him only playing a portion, how do we know he hasn't chopped and screwed the tape to make it sound like my client confessed?"

The judge scowled. "Mr. Ford, this is a bond revocation hearing, not a trial, and I don't want to be here all day. I grant permission to play the portion in which he confessed."

Again, Matt felt his body tense up. He didn't like where this was going, and he had a feeling that he wouldn't be going home today.

Chapter Eleven

The courtroom was silent as the DA prepared to play the tape of Matt's 'confession.'

Matt wiped his sweaty hands on his pants just as his voice rang out, echoing through the courtroom.

"Crap. This *is* all my fault. If that's conspiracy, then I'm guilty."

As the courtroom stirred with a buzzing noise, the judge pounded his gavel. "That's enough. Order in the court. I want silence."

Matt frantically looked at Ford. "That's not the whole thing. They messed with it. It's out of context. There was a lot of other stuff in between that."

Matt's heart sunk seeing his attorney's face. Ford looked like a child who had just seen the boogeyman under his bed.

"Uh... Judge Roberts," Ford stuttered. "Just as I suspected, that tape has been altered. While those are my client's words, entire sentences have been cut, which changes the context of his intention. This is *not* a confession."

Judge Roberts looked at the district attorney. "Mr. Simmons, has this tape been edited?"

"With all due respect, your honor, the tape has only been altered to capture the snippet of time in which Mr. Grant confesses. As I said before, it was a long interrogation, but the quintessence of this confession is authentic."

Judge Roberts held up his hand and closed his eyes. He rubbed his head. When he opened his eyes, he looked at Matt directly.

"Mr. Grant, I think this conspiracy to commit murder is a bunch of malarky, and coupled with your testimony that you didn't sign a waiver of rights, I'm not willing to verify the validity of this confession, either. However, these charges *are* serious crimes, and this is not a trial. Today, my only job is to determine whether you would be a threat to yourself or others until a trial commences. At the very least, you *did* meet with Mr. Ware, who has a history of criminal behavior. So, given the nature of these accusations, I have decided to err on the side of caution and revoke your bond. Please understand that this bond revocation is not a declaration of your guilt. I believe in our justice system. I've dedicated my life to it, and I am confident that you will receive a fair trial. I wish you the very best."

When the judge pounded his gavel and moved onto to the next order of business, all the blood drained from

Matt's face, and the thumping of his heart drowned out all the other sounds in the courtroom.

"Matt. Matt. Matt? Are you okay?" Ford patted Matt's back.

Matt shook his head. "No."

"Okay. You have to stand up. Go with the officer, now. Do you want a sip of water?"

Matt ignored his attorney, stood, and followed the officer.

***

Sleep. Eat. Shower. Repeat. Matt's days became an endless cycle of monotonous routine. He quit asking questions because they all went unanswered. Instead, he just waited. And waited. And waited. Occasionally, Ford visited Matt and told him that he had nothing to worry about—that the prosecution didn't have enough evidence to convict Matt at trial. And Matt clung to that hope—the promise of justice, the assurance that he would finally be vindicated, that his innocence would finally be divulged.

He thought about Amanda often, and at night, when he was supposed to be sleeping, he wept, wondering if she missed him as much as he missed her. When he finally succumbed to sleep, he saw her running to him, embracing him, telling him that she loved him. Those dreams maintained his sanity.

Three months after his bond revocation hearing, one of the officers escorted Matt to an interrogation room to meet with his attorney once again. Matt sat at a table and held a warm cup of coffee in his hand. And though the chair was just a metal foldout chair, the room was warm, and the coffee was mediocre, so Matt relished the time out of his cold, barren cell. Matt hoped that Ford was bringing news of a trial date.

The door opened, and Ford walked through, carrying a briefcase and looking as weaselly as ever.

"Matt," he said, extending his hand.

"Hi Jack," Matt said, standing to shake Ford's hand.

"How are you doing today?" he asked.

"Same old, same old," Matt replied. "I used to say that a lot, but now that I'm in here, it gives it a whole new meaning. It's literally the same old thing every day. Sometimes I feel like I'm gonna lose my mind."

"I know it's hard," Ford said, sitting opposite of Matt at the table.

"I hope you have some good news for me. A trial date, hopefully? The sooner we can get to trial, the sooner I can get outta here, right?"

"Well, uh. Actually, I'm not coming to talk about the trial. I'm... um... coming to tell you that William is suing you... you and your mother, actually."

"Suing me?" Matt asked. "Suing me for what?"

"Well, um... the lawsuit pretty much says that you stole his money and gave it to your mama. That's why he's suing you and her, both."

"Jesus. I don't have his freaking money. How can he sue me for something I haven't been convicted of?"

"Well, that's the thing. It might not even go to court. We'll have a hearing first to determine if there's enough evidence to proceed with the civil proceedings."

"So, we'll pretty much have a trial before the actual trial?"

"Um. Well, yeah. I guess you could say that. But the good news is that everything you say can be held against you during your criminal trial," Ford said as he nervously twirled the pen in his hand.

"How in the heck is that good news?" Matt asked.

Ford laughed. "You don't have to say anything. You can plead the 5th amendment. They'll have to give a deposition and present their evidence. This gives us an opportunity to see what they've got—and to see what direction they may be taking with the criminal trial."

"There *is* no evidence against me because I didn't do it," Matt said, running his hand through his hair.

Ford shuffled through some papers he pulled out of his briefcase. "Yeah, well, uh… it'll still let us hear their side of the story…"

"Yeah, but if they're suing me, can't I countersue? They've accused me of something terrible. Not only have I lost business, this has ruined my reputation."

Ford's eyes lit up. "Yeah. I, um… well, I was going to suggest that. Of course, that'll be more work for me…"

"Which means more money, right?"

"Well… uh…"

"It's fine," Matt said. "I can give my mom power of attorney, and she can make sure you get your money," Matt said. "Honestly, I just want all this done. If it costs me my life savings to get my life back, then so be it."

"Okay. I'll talk to your mother about the power of attorney, and I'll go ahead and file the countersuit," Ford said.

"What about the conspiracy to commit murder?" Matt asked. "Any update on that?"

"Oh yea," Ford said, beaming. "They dropped those charges."

"They dropped the charges, and you didn't tell me? Were you even going to mention that to me if I hadn't of asked?" Matt said, his voice rising.

The smile disappeared from Ford's face. "Um, yeah. Well, I just received the paperwork about that last week. It was... uh... it was on my list of items to discuss with you."

Matt took another sip of coffee. "So, does that mean I can go back home until the criminal trial starts? Since they dropped the other charges?"

"No," Ford said. "Afraid it doesn't work that way. The bond revocation is permanent, so uh... well... you know..."

"Yeah. I know. They charged me with a bogus crime so I'd have to sit in jail until trial—and because the courts are all backed up, who freaking knows when the trial will actually be scheduled. *And* William's' suing me and my seventy-three-year-old mother for money that I *didn't* steal from him. You're just full of good news today."

Ford frowned and started to put his papers back into his briefcase. "I know it's difficult, Matt. I understand, but I'm pretty confident that they don't have anything, so, as I've told you before, all this is a technicality—an unfortunate, miserable technicality, but after you're found non-guilty, you can go back to your normal life, and all this will just be like a bad nightmare."

Matt took another sip of his coffee. *I don't think life will ever be normal again,* he thought. "Can we just sit here a little while longer?" Matt asked. "Let me finish my coffee?"

"Of course," Ford said with a smile.

***

As soon as Matt entered the courtroom, he saw William sitting at a table close to the judge's bench with his lawyer, who wore an expensive suit with a gold tie clip. William looked up at Matt, and when their eyes locked, William gave Matt a sardonic smile. Matt shook his head and sat down beside his lawyer at their table.

"Remember," Ford said. "You say nothing other than 'I plead the 5th.'"

"Yeah, but I've been thinking. Doesn't that make me sound guilty? I mean, you plead the 5th so you won't incriminate yourself, but I'm innocent, so I can't incriminate myself for something I didn't do."

"You *can* incriminate yourself because they'll twist your words. Just trust me. Plead the 5th."

"Okay," Matt agreed.

When the judge entered, Matt was disappointed to see that it wasn't the gray-haired judge with sympathetic eyes from his bond-revocation hearing. This judge had black hair and tan, leathery skin. The deep lines around his mouth set his lips in a permanent frown.

"What happened to the other judge? The one I had before?" Matt whispered to his attorney.

"I don't know, but I would've rather had him. That's Benjamin Wilson. He's known for being callous."

"Great," Matt said. "That's just great."

"Don't worry about it. You're innocent, remember? This is all for show—a way for William Carson to make everyone feel sorry for him."

Matt nodded and looked down at his hands.

The judge cleared his throat. "Okay. We're going to get through this quickly. We're just getting depositions today, so I'm going to get right to it. Mr. Ford, I assume your client isn't going to give a deposition?"

Ford stood. "Yes, sir. Mr. Grant pleads the 5th."

"Okay. Mr. Grant," the judge said, looking at Matt. "I need to hear it from you, sir. Are you willing to answer questions for today's deposition?"

Matt looked at Ford, who nodded his head reassuringly. "I plead the 5th amendment, Sir."

"Okay," the judge said. "Mr. Anderson, we can start with Mr. Carson, if that's okay with you."

"Yes, sir," Mr. Anderson said. "Mr. Ford, are you prepared to take the deposition?"

"My colleague, Tom Freeland, will be taking the deposition, sir."

"Okay," the judge said. "Let's get on with it."

After William was sworn in, Matt looked up at him, trying to make eye contact, but William averted his eyes, refusing to look at Matt.

"State your name, please," Mr. Freeland said.

"Jerry William Carson."

"Mr. Carson, my name is Tom Freeland. I'm one of the lawyers for Matt Grant. And I'll be taking your deposition. Do you know what a deposition is?"

"Yes, sir."

As the legal talk continued, Matt looked down at the empty legal pad in front of him and let his mind wander. *How did it ever come to this?* he thought, and he sighed heavily. Matt half-listened as Mr. Freeland asked William about his house, the safe, and the contents of the safe. When the tone of Mr. Freeland's voice rose, Matt paid closer attention.

"I walked out in the yard and looked where I felt they had backed a wrecker in. I think they were going to pull the safe through the wall, so I was looking at tracks, black marks on the pavement, looking for any kind of signs—cigarette butts, Coke bottles, et cetera, anything that could be used to determine who did the robbery," William said.

"Where did you get the idea that they were going to back a wrecker in?" Mr. Freeland asked.

"Because my house had been broken into several years prior. They found the safe in there and had made the statement that they would be back—that they would get the safe the next time they come—that they would jerk it through the wall."

"Who is 'they'? You said 'they' made the statement that they'd be back."

"The FBI."

"Mr. Carson, the FBI certainly didn't break into your house. Who is the 'they' that broke into your house years ago?"

"I don't know, but the FBI told me they'd get the safe next time."

"The FBI told you that whoever broke into your house before would be back?"

"Yes sir," William replied.

"Why was the FBI involved in this case?"

"I don't know. I guess they thought I was important." William smiled.

"Well, did the police ever arrest anyone in connection with this crime?"

"Not that I'm aware of," William said.

"Then how did the FBI agent know that the perpetrators would be back?"

"I don't know," William said.

Matt stopped listening and let his mind wander again. *The FBI tells you that somebody who broke into your house would be back for the safe, and still, you accuse me of stealing your money? He's so full of it.*

Matt folded his hands and breathed a sigh of relief when William's deposition was done. Seeing him sitting up there on the stand was making Matt sick to his stomach.

After William gave his deposition, Diana testified. The lawyer asked her many of the same questions that he asked William, and though Matt had trouble focusing, he made a list on his legal pad of the items he found interesting from their testimonies.

> 1. They had never counted the money in the safe before, but 10 days before they went on vacation, Diana supposedly

counted the money and wrote the amount on the inside of the safe.

2.	Then, William supposedly added money to the safe 'after' Diana counted and recorded the amount.

3.	They didn't set the alarm before they went on vacation.

4.	This was the first extended vacation they'd taken in 30 years, and their life savings was stolen.

5.	This was the first time they had ever been to the cabin in Colorado, but Sorbo had stayed in their cabin twice before.

6.	Shelia was 'in charge' of making sure the gate was locked.

7.	They both said that Sorbo and Greer had only been in their house a couple

> of times, and neither of them knew about the safe. (<u>**DEFINITELY A LIE**</u>)
>
> 8. Diana believes I'm guilty because she heard my taped 'confession' at the bond revocation hearing.

Matt looked over his list. *This is ludicrous*, he thought. There were too many coincidences, and his heart sunk deep into his stomach. Matt had always thought he was being set up to take the fall for this crime, but for the first time, he wondered if William had orchestrated the whole burglary himself. *For the insurance money*, he thought. *If William had someone 'steal' the money and give him the money back, minus their cut, he could make a good profit by claiming insurance.* Matt shook his head to rid the thought from his head. *Surely, the Carsons wouldn't do that to me. But they **are** doing it. I'm sitting in jail while they're trying to make even more money by suing me.*

The weight of it all fell on Matt, and he looked down at his paper, trying to prevent an inevitable sob. Then, a thought crossed his mind, and he felt like he was going to vomit. *What if Shelia was in on it, too? What if the plan was always to implicate me—to make a family profit at my expense?*

Chapter Twelve

Sorbo was up next, and Matt was all ears. He wanted to hear what this crook had to say.

"Tell us what happened," the lawyer said. "How did y'all break into Mr. Carson's house?"

"Do I go through the—"

Yes. Just tell us the story."

Sorbo sighed and said, "We met at Danny's house that night."

"Let's clarify for the record. Danny is Daniel Greer?"

"Yeah."

"Okay. Go on."

"Well, then we rode over there," Sorbo said.

"Who rode over there? You and Daniel Greer?"

"No, Danny dropped us off, me and Justin Hinder."

"Dropped you off at William Carson's house?"

"Yeah," Sorbo replied.

"And where did Mr. Greer go?"

"I don't know. He was supposed to come back and pick us up in an hour."

"An hour? That's a long time for a robbery," the attorney said.

"Well, we knew they were on vacation, so we weren't worried about them coming home or nothing. There wasn't a rush."

"Okay. Continue, please."

"Well, when we got there, we stopped and got our stuff out. Right there at the gate, we hopped a fence to get down into the pasture and went all the way across. William lives on the back side of the pasture, kind of between the highway and the county road. Then, we went up to William's house, and we just looked... took our time and looked around. We couldn't find the keys to the tractor. That was the original plan."

"What was the original plan?" the lawyer asked.

"The hay fork of the tractor. We were just going to put it through the... uh... where the safe was in that side room, just stick it through the brick wall."

"Then what?" the attorney asked.

"Then, we were going to just pull the safe out of the brick wall—with the tractor."

"But you couldn't find the keys to the tractor?" the lawyer asked.

"Yes, sir."

"Why would you assume that you'd be able to find the keys to the tractor? After all, Mr. Carson was on vacation. Wouldn't he have stored the keys to his equipment inside his house?"

"Well... uh... they were supposed to be... I mean... William usually just left them under the mat."

"Okay," the lawyer said. "Let's take a detour for a moment. How many times have you been to Mr. Carson's house?"

"Lord, I couldn't count. Many times."

"More than 50?"

"Probably," Sorbo replied.

"Okay. Let's go back to the original plan. The plan was to ram the wall with a tractor and then retrieve the safe?"

"Yeah. We were going to get a chain from William's shop and pull the safe out."

"So, the shop was open?"

"It was supposed to... well, I mean, he ain't never locked it before," Sorbo said.

"Then what were you going to do with the safe after you retrieved it?"

"Load it up onto one of William's service trucks. They keys were supposed to be... well, um... like I said...the keys are always in the truck... under the mat."

"So, you were going take the safe away in the truck? You were going to steal the truck, too?"

"Yeah. Well, we would'a brought it back."

"So, where were you going to take the safe?"

"We were going to take it back to Danny's house to open it."

"So, let me get this straight. You were going to plow through the wall, rip the safe out, put it in William's truck, and take the truck and the safe to Danny's house. So again, the original plan was to steal the safe *and* a truck."

"Naw. We was just gonna borrow the truck. We was supposed to take the truck back after we dropped off the safe."

"Can you clarify what you mean by saying 'we were supposed to take the truck back'? Who said you were supposed to take the truck back?"

"Oh... uh... that was the plan that... uh... that Matt came up with."

"Okay. But you didn't have the key to the tractor, so what did you do next?"

"We grabbed some sledgehammers from William's shop and tried to knock down the wall."

"And when you say 'we,' you're referring to you and Justin Hinder, right?"

"Yes, sir."

"And were you able to break the wall?"

"No. It wasn't happening," Sorbo said.

So, what did you do next?"

"Well, Hinder got some tools and popped the door open," Sorbo said. "And then, the burglar alarm went off."

"The alarm went off?" the lawyer asked. Mr. and Mrs. Carson just testified that they didn't set the alarm before they left for vacation."

"They did? Oh... well... uh... yeah... I mean... I don't know how it got set, then."

"Well, what did you do when the alarm went off?"

"Uh... Matt had given us the code to the alarm. I remembered because the numbers were straight down, 2580. Anyway, I was going to put in the code to turn it off, but it quit beeping on its own."

"The alarm just turned off by itself?"

"Yeah."

"Okay, well, what did you do next?"

"We went in the shed and got some tools to break into the safe. Then, Hinder beat the door off it."

"And you took all the money out of the safe. What did you do with it?"

"We took it back to Danny's house. We split fifty thousand up, but we left the rest there so Matt could get it later."

"You left the rest of it there?"

"Yeah."

"Okay. We'll come back to that. Tell me. Why did you choose fifty thousand for yourselves?" the attorney asked.

"That's what was promised to us."

"By Mr. Grant?"

"Yeah."

"So, Mr. Grant got to keep the rest?"

"Well, uh... no.... he was uh... gonna wash it and then give us some more."

"Wash it?" the lawyer asked. "For the record, can you explain what you mean by that?"

"Well, uh, Matt was going to use the money... take it to the casino, and that way, he'd be getting new bills, not the same money we stole from the safe."

"And what was the purpose of that?"

"Well, uh... we uh... William might've known the serial numbers on the bills or something like that. If we got different bills, then they couldn't trace it back to us. That's what Matt said."

"We know that Mr. Carson gambles from his testimony. To your knowledge, is Mr. Grant a gambler?"

"Well... uh... no... I don't know... I ain't ever heard him talking about it before."

"So, as far as you know, he's not a regular gambler."

"I don't know," Sorbo said.

"Okay. Let's change directions again. When was the last time you had a meeting with Matt before the robbery?"

"Um, just a couple of days before."

"And what did you talk about during that meeting?"

"He just told me that everybody was going to be out of town."

"Now, had Matt arranged for you to get together with Justin Hinder and Daniel Greer at that time?"

"No. Well, it was kind of... I don't know... I don't know... you don't know what I'm doing. As long as I don't know and I don't see you, I don't know. As long as you don't see me and I don't know... you don't know what I'm doing, you can't... you can't say what I'm doing. It was kind of like, if you don't know, I don't know, you know? But when it's all said and done, I'm going to get the last laugh."

"Mr. Sorbo, it's difficult to decipher what you were trying to say there. However, it *could* be interpreted as you saying that *you* set Matt up to take the fall for your crime."

"No. I meant that Matt was going to get the last laugh, not me."

"Okay. But there's no proof that you had that meeting with Mr. Grant. How do we know that you're not making it up?"

"Well, um... I think... um, well, Matt sent me a text that night... pretty much to say that everything was all clear."

"So, you're saying that Mr. Grant texted you to tell you that you were good to go—to break into Mr. Carson's home?"

"Yeah. I... uh... think so. Well, maybe he called me... or I called him. I don't know, but yeah, I got the all-clear from Matt," Sorbo said, stuttering.

"We can check your phone records, but back to the story. Who actually took the money from the safe?"

"Justin Hinder did."

"Then what did you do next? Be specific."

"Then, we walked back to where Greer had dropped us off and waited for him to pick us up."

"Now, in your statement, you said that you had surgery the next day. A moment ago, you also mentioned that you left some money there for Mr. Grant to pick up."

"Yeah."

"And you said you and Mr. Hinder took fifty thousand for yourselves. Was that the only amount you were supposed to get in this deal?"

"Naw. I done told you. Matt was gonna wash it and give us some more."

"Why did you take the fifty thousand that night, then? Why not take more?"

"Uh.... we... uh... well, we decided we were going to wait for Matt to get his share before we got our money. Hinder said that Matt told him to divvy it out in small amounts, not to look suspicious."

"So now you're saying that Hinder also spoke to Matt about the plan. I thought you were the only one who knew Matt personally."

"Well, uh, yeah. I think I might've introduced Hinder to Matt. Maybe Hinder was at one of the meetings with Matt. I can't remember."

"I see. And did anyone divvy some money out for you the next day? Did anyone bring some more money by your house?" the attorney asked.

"Uh... well.. uh... there was four-thousand... well, forty-five-hundred dollars that showed up in my Jeep, I think... in five-dollar bills."

"It just showed up in your Jeep?"

"Yeah. In the console. In a little brown paper sack," Sorbo said.

"So, you don't know who gave you that money?"

"I asked Matt about it. He said it was free money. He said, 'Hey, everybody likes free money.'"

"You asked Mr. Grant about this? Was that in person or by phone?"

"I... uh... I can't remember. On the phone, maybe."

"So, the 4,500 dollars and the 50,000 dollars you split with Mr. Hinder was the only money you received from this burglary?"

"Well, yeah. I mean... uh... I was supposed to get more later... after... I was going to get my cut later."

"But you never did?"

"No. I was arrested."

"Well, what happened to the money?"

"I uh... I don't know. I mean... some of it... well, there was... I'm not sure."

"Okay. Let's go back to your earlier statement. You said that you left some of the money there for Mr. Grant to pick up later. Is that correct?"

"Uh... yeah."

"Where did you leave the money?"

"I don't know."

What do you mean, you don't know?"

"Hinder had the money, and I don't know where he left it."

"But you were with him. Didn't you see what he did with it?"

"It was dark, and I wasn't paying attention."

"I see. Now, Mr. Sorbo, I want to talk to you about your statements to the police. It seems that your story has changed quite a few times."

"Well, uh. It mighta changed, just because I couldn't remember stuff."

"I see, but in one statement, didn't you tell the police that you were the lookout person? That you were nearly a mile away, and your job was to let Greer and Hinder know if any cars came by?"

"Um. I don't know. Did I say that?"

"Yes, sir. According to police interviews, that's what you said."

"Well, I might've just said that because I thought I would get in more trouble if the cops knew that I was there—at the house."

Okay. Let's change directions once again. Would you say that Matt is a jealous man—in his relationships?"

"Yeah. He heard his wife was messing around with a cop, and he asked me to check it out—to follow the guy—to spy for him."

"I see," the lawyer said. "Well, are you aware that Mr. Grant's ex-wife had been intimate with Mr. Greer?"

"Uh. Well, yeah. I knew that," Sorbo stammered.

"Well, if Mr. Grant was a jealous man, why would he beseech the services of a man who had slept with his wife?"

"Well, uh... they were getting a divorce, and that happened a long time ago... before they were married... I think... he... uh... yeah."

Matt stopped listening and read back over the list he had written on his steno pad.

> 1.   They had never counted the money in the safe before, but 10 days before they went on vacation, Diana counted the money and wrote the amount on the inside of the safe.
>
> 2.   Then, William supposedly added money to the safe 'after' Diana counted and recorded the amount.
>
> 3.   They didn't set the alarm before they went on vacation. <u>Sorbo said that the</u>

<u>alarm was on—and that I gave him the code to disarm the safe but that the alarm went off by itself. What an idiot.</u>

4. This was the first extended vacation they'd taken in 30 years, and their life savings was stolen.

5. This was the first time they had ever been to the cabin in Colorado, but Sorbo had stayed in their cabin twice before.

6. Shelia was 'in charge' of making sure the gate was locked.

<u>William and Diana</u>

7. ~~They~~ both said that Sorbo and Greer had only been in there house a couple of times, and neither of them knew about the safe. (<u>Definitely a lie</u>). <u>Sorbo says that he's good friends with William and that he's been in their house many times.</u>

8.　Diana believes I'm guilty because she heard my taped 'confession' at the bond revocation hearing.

9.　Sorbo said it was my idea to 'wash' the money at the casino. I don't gamble, but William lives in that casino. <u>FISHY</u>.

10.　Sorbo said I texted or called him the night of the robbery. <u>DID NOT HAPPEN.</u>

11.　Sorbo is barely making any sense. <u>**SURELY, HIS TESTIMONY CANNOT BE USED AS EVIDENCE.**</u>

12.　Money just showed up in his Jeep? <u>WTF?</u>

13.　I never asked Sorbo to spy on anyone for me. <u>LIAR</u>. And I would never associate with someone who slept with the <u>MOTHER OF MY CHILD.</u>

Matt looked over the list as Sorbo continued to stutter and lie on the witness stand. He shook his head and thought, *how in the hell am I in jail for this crap? I wasn't there. There's no proof that I even met up with these idiots, much less planned a robbery with them. The more I hear, the more I'm convinced that William set this up himself just to frame me. And now, he's relying on his connections to make sure it sticks—even though there isn't any evidence.*

When Matt exhaled, he didn't even realize he was holding his breath, but the sharp intake of oxygen cleared his brain.

My lawyers say it's an open-and-shut case. There's no way they can pin this on me. Ford said this is just a formality. Everything's going to be okay. Everything's going to be okay.

He repeated the mantra in his head over and over and over.

Chapter Thirteen

Back in jail, the hours droned on again, filled with monotonous routine. It was difficult to keep track of days, and each morning, he prayed his lawyer would arrive and tell him that they'd set a trial date. As far as he was concerned, the sooner the case went to trial, the sooner he'd be exonerated.

One morning, an officer came to his cell and announced, "Grant, your lawyer's here to see you. Follow me, please."

Matt smiled, thinking that Ford had finally come to tell him the date of the trial. When they got to the room, the officer looked at Matt and asked, "You want a cup of coffee?"

Matt smiled. He'd been there long enough for them to anticipate his needs. "Yes, sir. Thank you." Then, Matt turned to Ford, sitting in a chair beside the small table. "Mr. Ford, I sure am glad to see you this morning. I'm guessing you came to tell me that they've set a court date for the trial, right?"

"No, I'm afraid not, Matt. I'm sorry. But I do have a development that I need to share with you. Have a seat."

Ford looked more like a weasel than ever, and his face was pale, but red splotches dotted his neck.

Matt sat down tentatively. "This doesn't sound like good news," he said.

"Well, no. I guess it's not," Ford said, and he broke into a coughing fit.

"Are you okay?" Matt asked.

"Yeah. Yeah. Allergies. I'm fine," Ford said.

Just then, the officer brought in Matt's cup of coffee and sat it on the table in front of him. "Thanks again, Man. I really appreciate it," Matt said.

The officer nodded and left the room, and Matt turned his attention back to Ford.

"Well, see, the police have been investigating the case more, and they've found some new information. It seems that Sorbo and Hinder took money out of Mr. Carson's safe and put the majority of it in a culvert for you to retrieve later."

"A culvert?" Matt asked.

"Yes. A culvert off the back side of Mr. Carson's property."

Matt shook his head and laughed. "You can't be serious. Wouldn't the money get wet or get washed away in a culvert?"

"Um... well, yeah. I suppose so, but supposedly, the money was in a plastic bag, I guess, to protect it from water."

"This came from Sorbo?" Matt asked.

"Yes. Sorbo's story has changed a number of times. At first, he testified that Hinder left the money for you but that he was unaware of the details."

Matt rolled his eyes. "Yeah. I remember that."

"He now says that he lied about that part—that he and Hinder left the money in a culver together, per your instructions. The police have been out there to investigate the culvert." Ford slid a photo across the table to Matt. "As you can see, this culvert is easily approachable. It'd be easy to put money in there, and it'd be easy to retrieve that money at a later date."

Matt looked at the photo of a police officer standing in front of a large culvert. Then, he looked back up at Ford. "Well, this is obviously another lie. What is this—the fourth time that Sorbo's story has changed?"

"Um, well, yes, but Mr. Sorbo is being very cooperative in working with the police."

"Yeah. I guess so. He robbed a friend of his. I'd be cooperative, too, if I was guilty. Anyway, what does this have to do with me?" Matt asked.

Ford's eyes narrowed, and he took a deep breath. "I'm going to need more money to continue working on this case," he said.

Matt almost spit out his coffee. "What?" Matt asked. "We already agreed on a price. I've already given you the money upfront for this case—and for the countersuit we filed."

"I know, but with new developments, this case is getting more complicated, and to proceed, I'm going to need to be compensated adequately."

Matt shook his head. "No. No. You can't do this. You can't agree to a fee and then change it later. I signed a contract with you."

"I need fifty-thousand more, and if you don't come up with it, then I'm off the case."

"Fifty thousand?" Matt shouted. "Are you crazy? I'm sure they've frozen my bank accounts by now, and besides, I'm not working anymore. I don't have that kind of cash."

Ford narrowed his eyes again. "You have the culvert money."

A scowl transformed Matt's face. "The culvert money? Are you serious? I've told you from the beginning that I didn't do this. I never had anything to do with this robbery, and I don't have any damn culvert money."

Ford flashed a wily grin. "Sure. If that's how you want to play it, Matt. In any case, I've been in touch with your mother. She has agreed to mortgage her house to pay for your attorney's fees, and you've already given her power of attorney, so the money shouldn't be an issue, even if you *do* want to keep the culvert money all to yourself."

Matt slammed his hand on the table and stood up. "Damn, it. That's enough. You weaselly-ass crook. You're really going to try to take advantage of a sick, old woman like this? Why, I ought to..."

"You ought to what?" Ford asked.

Hearing the noise from Matt hitting the table, an officer opened the door and poked his head in. "Everything okay in here?" he asked.

Ford smiled at the officer. "Everything's fine. Mr. Grant's just a little upset regarding some new evidence, but we're okay. Please give us a few more minutes," he said.

The officer nodded. "Let us know if you need us," he said and closed the door.

Ford turned back to Matt. "Look, I'm all you got, as far as attorneys go. William Carson and his cronies have drug your name through the mud, and no other attorney in this town will touch this case with a ten-foot pole, just because of who Carson is—and because most people think you're guilty."

"But you said this was a slam-shut case."

"Yeah, well, you can't ignore the court of public opinion, and I hate to tell you, if you have a trial in this county, then the jury has already found you guilty."

"I can't allow my mother to mortgage her house. She barely makes it as it is, not without my help. She can't afford a mortgage payment every month," Matt said, his voice lower now, filled with despair.

Ford retrieved the photo from the table, put it back into his folder, and shut the file. "Fine. I'll contact the courts and let them know that you'll need to be assigned a public defender—some overworked, unsympathetic asshole who's probably been kissing William Carson's ass for years."

Tears filled Matt's eyes.

Ford stood and walked to the door. "Good luck, Mr. Grant. Hope you enjoy spending the rest of your life in prison."

"Wait," Matt said.

Ford turned around and smiled.

***

After Ford got his money, he continued to update Matt on the police investigation, which sounded like a lot more malarky to Matt. He still couldn't believe he was sitting in jail for a crime he didn't commit, and on top of that, this whole situation was putting his mother in a financial bind, and they still hadn't scheduled a trial date.

Matt had come to hate Ford. He despised his thin-lipped smile, his whiny voice, and his jittery manner, but then again, Matt didn't think he had any other choice. He needed a lawyer because it was obvious that the police were trying to pin this on Matt—whether they had any evidence or not. But Matt was getting frustrated. He was rotting away in jail while the world outside his cell moved on unapologetically.

He missed Amanda. He hadn't seen her since he had been arrested, not that he expected Shelia to bring her to visit him. The only real information he received about the case was filtered through his weasel lawyer, but Matt had deduced that Shelia was just as culpable in framing Matt as her father. It killed him to think about what they were telling Amanda. He just hoped that he'd eventually get to set the record straight with her.

The meetings with Ford were bittersweet. Even though he dreaded seeing that swindler's pudgy face, it was the only time he got to break routine, leave his cell, and drink a good cup of coffee.

In today's meeting, he was venting his frustration. "I don't see why you can't do something about this. I mean, they put a bogus charge on me so I couldn't get out on bail, and I've been sitting in this damn jail cell for months, waiting for a trial that still hasn't been scheduled. How is that fair? When I'm found innocent, are they going to pay me back for everything I've been through? Are they going to compensate me for my missed work? Hell no. I'm literally missing the opportunity to see my daughter grow up, and God knows what she thinks of me now, considering her mother and grandfather have convinced everyone in town that I'm a thief. It's all bullshit," Matt said.

Ford squinted his eyes and said, "Well, there *is* another way."

"What?" Matt asked.

"I could try to get you a deal. If you plead guilty, then we don't have to wait on a trial."

"But I'm not guilty," Matt said. "I keep telling you that, and I know you don't believe me because you keep bringing up that damn culvert money, like I've got a stash of cash hidden away somewhere, but I don't. I'm innocent."

"Yeah, but let's say you get a deal, and you're offered a light sentence. You might spend less time in jail with a sentence than you would just waiting for a trial."

Matt thought about it for a moment, and then he shook his head. "No. I can't do that. I'd be a convicted felon, and besides, then Amanda really *would* think I was guilty. I mean, she probably already does, based on what her Mama's telling her, but as far as I'm concerned, I need to maintain my innocence so that I can reiterate to her that I had nothing to do with this."

"Your decision. It's just a thought. I can't make them schedule the trial, so I don't know how long you'll be here. Honestly, it could be a year or more."

Matt took a sip of his coffee and thought about it some more. "No, I can't," he said aloud, mostly to himself. "I've already put Mama through enough, and if I plead guilty, then she might start to doubt my innocence—and I don't want people thinking she has a criminal son. No. I can't do it. It'd be a lie. I mean, I can't help but be curious—to see what kind of deal they'd offer, especially since they *have* to know I'm innocent, but no. No. I can't plead guilty, no matter how good of a deal they offer."

"I've talked to your Mama. She thinks the world revolves around you. There's no way she'd doubt your innocence, even if you *did* plead guilty. I could explain to her why you're doing it, but like I said, it's your choice."

◆

Chapter Fourteen

After another restless night on his uncomfortable cot, Matt stood, went to his little sink, and splashed some water on his face. He was just about to start reading a book his mom sent him when an officer rapped on his cell.

"Hey, Grant," he said. "Got some bad news."

"What?" Matt asked, and the hair on the back of his neck stood up. *What else could happen?* he thought.

"It's your mom. She's in the hospital."

"Is she okay? What happened?" Matt asked.

"I don't know," he replied. "Your lawyer called, said to relay the information to you. He's on his way here. I assume he'll give you an update when he arrives. Sit tight. We'll let you know when he gets here."

Matt sat on his cot and put his head in his hands. *Why in the hell would Ford just call and tell me she's in the hospital without giving me any more information? That shiesty little asshole. God, I hope Mama's okay. Dear Lord, please let her be okay. Please, please, please. I'm begging you. I know I've prayed for myself a lot here lately, but I don't care what happens to me—as long as Mama's okay. She doesn't deserve any of this.*

Tears filled Matt's eyes again, and he felt fear creep up into his throat. He stood and paced the small space in his cell, wondering how long he'd have to wait before Ford would arrive.

Then, he sat down again. Frustrated and scared, he picked up his Bible. *Oh, God. I need you now,* he prayed. Then, he closed his eyes and opened the Bible to a random section. Tears dropped down onto the page as he read.

Psalm 42
1 As the deer pants for streams of water,
   so my soul pants for you, my God.
2 My soul thirsts for God, for the living God.
   When can I go and meet with God?
3 My tears have been my food
   day and night,
while people say to me all day long,
   "Where is your God?"
4 These things I remember
   as I pour out my soul:
how I used to go to the house of God
under the protection of the Mighty One[d]
   with shouts of joy and praise
       among the festive throng.

5 Why, my soul, are you downcast?
   Why so disturbed within me?
     Put your hope in God,
       for I will yet praise him,
         my Savior and my God.

6 My soul is downcast within me;
   therefore I will remember you
   from the land of the Jordan,
the heights of Hermon—from Mount Mizar.

⁷ Deep calls to deep
  in the roar of your waterfalls;
all your waves and breakers
  have swept over me.

⁸ By day the Lord directs his love,
  at night his song is with me—
  a prayer to the God of my life.

⁹ I say to God my Rock,
  "Why have you forgotten me?
Why must I go about mourning,
  oppressed by the enemy?"
¹⁰ My bones suffer mortal agony
  as my foes taunt me,
saying to me all day long,
  "Where is your God?"

¹¹ Why, my soul, are you downcast?
  Why so disturbed within me?
Put your hope in God,
  for I will yet praise him,
  my Savior and my God.

Psalm 43

1 Vindicate me, my God,
  and plead my cause
  against an unfaithful nation.
Rescue me from those who are
  deceitful and wicked.
2 You are God my stronghold.
  Why have you rejected me?
Why must I go about mourning,
  oppressed by the enemy?
3 Send me your light and your faithful care,
  let them lead me;
let them bring me to your holy mountain,
  to the place where you dwell.
4 Then I will go to the altar of God,
  to God, my joy and my delight.
I will praise you with the lyre,
  O God, my God.

> 5 Why, my soul, are you downcast?
> Why so disturbed within me?
> Put your hope in God,
> for I will yet praise him,
> my Savior and my God.

Thank you, Lord, Matt thought. *Thank you for showing me that you haven't abandoned me. I've felt so alone, so hopeless.*

Suddenly, Matt felt a peace overcome him, and he knew his mother would be okay.

***

Matt held the cup of coffee with both hands, and he took a large gulp, trying to warm the coldness he felt in his bones. Though praying made him feel better, he was still anxious to hear about his mother.

"So, what's going on?" Matt asked. "Is she okay?"

"She's okay—for now. The doctors obviously wouldn't talk to me, but I was able to see her, and she told me that she has pneumonia. She was having a hard time catching her breath, and she called 911. The ambulance picked her up and took her to the hospital. They have her hooked up to an IV, and I'm assuming they're giving her antibiotics."

"Jesus," Matt said. "How'd she look?"

Ford shook his head and frowned. "Not good. Not good at all. Her coloring's off, and she looks feeble. I don't know. I think maybe she's lost some weight, but she told me to come see you—to tell you not to worry about her. She said she'd be fine."

Matt sighed. "She won't be fine. Not if I'm in here for much longer. She lives alone, and she doesn't have anybody to watch out for her. She had to take an ambulance to the hospital, for Christ's sake—and we both know she can't afford that."

"Calm down, Matt. She's got Medicare and insurance. They should cover most of the bill."

"That's not the point," Matt said. "She's out there, all alone, and she couldn't breathe, and she..." Matt tried to hold it in, but a sob escaped his lips. He wiped his tears and continued. "She's sick, and she was all alone. Usually, I'd be the one to be there—to help her, to take her to a doctor, to make sure she's taking her medicine. It's not fair. She shouldn't be alone."

"I know. I understand," Ford said. "It's not fair. It really isn't, but there's nothing we can do about it. Unless..."

"Unless what?" Matt asked.

"Unless you've reconsidered my proposition about pleading guilty."

"I already told you. I can't do that. I'm not guilty," Matt said.

"But we could get you out in a relatively short time. I've already talked to the DA, and he said…"

"You talked to the DA?" Matt asked incredulously. "Why did you do that? I told you I wasn't pleading guilty. You had no right to talk to the DA without my permission."

"Look, Matt. I'm just trying to help you out," Ford replied.

"That's bullshit, too, Ford. You've bled me and my mother dry, and if I plead guilty, then you can take all that money, be done with this case, and ride off into the sunset with my cash."

"That's not fair. I've been nice to your mother."

"Yeah. Forcing her to mortgage her house is really nice," Matt said sullenly.

"I'm not here to argue, Matt. I just wanted to give you an update on your mom, but the fact remains. Your mom is sick, and every day, she's getting older and frailer. I'm sorry to point that out, but it's true. And your daughter, well, every day you're in here is a day without you—a day where she's growing up, having new experiences, and enjoying life—*minus* her father. How long before she forgets you completely?"

"You really are a son of a bitch," Matt said.

"No. I'm just being honest with you. Now, I know you don't want to plead guilty because you claim you're innocent..."

"I don't *claim* I'm innocent; I *am* innocent," Matt yelled.

Ford held up his hand. "Let me finish. Let's say you're innocent, and because of pride or honor or whatever the hell you want to call it, you're willing to sit your ass here in jail until this goes to trial—and even then, there's a chance that they'll still find you guilty. Sure, they don't have much evidence, but as you've seen, the people in charge—the important people—well, they seem to think you've done this—or at the very least, they want you to take the fall for it. And this is a small county. Everybody's already heard about this case, so jurors will pretty much have their minds made up before they even get to trial. I can't guarantee you a non-guilty verdict. But, with a guilty plea, I can guarantee a light at the end of the tunnel—a way out of all this mess."

Matt blew out a breath of air. "I can't. I just can't plead guilty to something I didn't do. It's not right. I'd feel like a phony, and while you may call it pride, I call it integrity."

"Well," Ford said. "There is another option, too."

"What?" Matt asked.

"An Alford plea."

"What the hell is that?" Matt asked.

"In an Alford plea, you still plead guilty, but you maintain your innocence. You're basically saying that you think there's enough evidence to convict you, even though you didn't actually commit the crime."

"But I'd still be a convicted felon?"

"Well, yeah, but you can also get this over with—serve a sentence and be done with it—all without saying that you committed the crime."

"Well, what about the sentence? What would it be?"

"I don't know, Matt. I can't give you a specific answer, but I can meet with the DA, who could talk to the judge on your behalf, to request a lighter sentence, if you agree to plead guilty. After all, it saves everybody a lot of time and effort."

"So, would you refund some of the money I gave you—considering your job would be over?"

Ford laughed. "No. I'm afraid it doesn't work that way."

"Of course not," Matt said. He sighed. "I don't know."

"It's a win-win," Ford said. "You get what you want—a specific amount of time to serve, hopefully, a reduced sentence. And the DA gets what he wants—a conviction."

"Yeah, but I'd still be *convicted*—for a crime I didn't commit."

"Yes, but you'd maintain your innocence. Let's be honest. You don't care what the world thinks about you, but you *do* care about your mother and your daughter. You'd be resolving this issue and still letting them know that you didn't do this. Instead of being stuck in this stupid hole, you can serve your time, get out, and finally get on with your life. You could take care of your mother, Matt. She needs you. And Amanda? How do you think she feels with you being gone? A daughter *needs* her father."

Angry tears filled Matt's eyes. "Don't do that. Don't talk about my daughter. You have no right to say her name or use her against me—especially after you pretty much blackmailed me into paying you a small fortune."

Ford put his hands up and said, "Sorry. Like I said, I'm just trying to help—to do what's best for you."

Matt wiped the tears from his eyes. "I've made it very clear that I don't like you, and I think you're a crook who has taken advantage of me *and* my mother." He paused. "But you're right. My mother needs me, and Amanda needs me." He paused again. "I'll do it."

Ford smiled. "Okay. Let me see if I can talk the DA into accepting an Alford plea."

Part Two
Deceptive Betrayal

Chapter Fifteen

As Diana Carson rustled through the kitchen, a delicious aroma swathed the house. She smiled when her husband, William, entered the kitchen and pecked her on the cheek with a kiss.

"Smells delicious," he said.

"Thanks, Dear. I'm making biscuits with the gravy you like. It'll be about thirty minutes before it's done, though."

"Okay, sounds good," William said. "I'm going to go confirm our reservations for the trip. Let me know when it's time to eat?" he said with a grin.

"Of course," she replied. "I can't wait for Colorado. I need a change in scenery."

"Me too, Hon," he replied as he walked toward his office.

Once in his office, William closed the door and engaged the lock. He sat at his desk, sighed, and held his head in his hands. After a brief moment of contemplation, William picked up the landline phone from his desk and dialed.

"Sorbo. It's William. I'm calling to confirm. Are you ready to execute the plan?"

As the caller replied, William rolled his eyes and shook his head.

"No. I want you to do this alone. It *has* to look like the two of you planned it. Just stick to the plan," William said, and he slammed the phone down on the receiver.

***

Savoring her chicken breast, Diana looked out at the mountains displayed before her. Based on Yelp reviews, she had chosen this restaurant for its picturesque windows that revealed mountain views from every seat. The reviews were right. The view was stunning, and the food was delicious, so she decided it was worth the exorbitant price.

"This view is beautiful," she said to herself. She took another bite and said, "William, you have to try a bite of this chicken. It's so good. It just melts in your mouth."

She looked up at her husband, who was staring absently out the window, though he didn't appear to be admiring the view. He showed no indication that he had heard her speaking to him.

"William. William? Did you hear me?"

"What? No. I'm sorry. I just spaced out there for a second. What'd you say?"

Diana frowned. "What's going on with you? We're in the most beautiful setting I've ever seen, and you've been distracted all week."

William smiled and patted her hand. "You're right. I'm sorry. I've just been thinking about work stuff, but all that can wait, right? I'll try to be more present. Now, what did you say?"

Diana looked skeptical. "I was just saying how good the chicken is. How's your steak?" She noticed that he had only taken a few bites.

"It's fine. Just fine," he said.

The waitress arrived, presenting a striking smile. "How are you guys doing? Can I get you anything else?"

"We're good. Thanks," William replied curtly.

As the waitress nodded and scooted away, Diana shot another concerned glance at her husband. "Something's obviously on your mind," she said. "Are you still fuming about Shelia and Matt?"

William started to take another bite of steak and then thought better of it. "Yeah. I still can't believe she decided to go on a trip with him. I thought they were done, and now they're dredging all this shit up again? He was out of our lives, and now, she's reeling him back in. She doesn't listen to a damn thing I say."

Diana took a sip of her wine and sighed. "We've talked about this. They have a child. Matt will never really be out of our lives completely because he's the father of our grandchild."

"Well, I don't have to like it," he said.

"I still don't know what you have against that boy. He's never been nothing but nice to us, and God knows I'd give my life for Shelia, but she probably wasn't easy to live with."

"She wasn't easy to live with? Come on. Matt thinks he knows everything, and he thinks he's better than everyone—including you and me. That nice-guy routine is just a façade. Shelia was miserable, and you know, I was all for them working it out, but he's the one that filed for divorce, and she was devastated. But after the divorce was final, it was like a weight was lifted from her shoulders. She was finally happy again, and now, she wants to invite that misery back into her life? It just pisses me off."

"She's a grown woman, William. A mother. We can't tell her what to do, and we certainly can't control her decisions."

"The hell I can't," William said.

"I've already told you. Stay out of it. Maybe they can work it out and get back together. If they do, is that really a bad thing? Amanda adores him, and he's a good father."

"No. Working it out *isn't* a good thing. Everybody in town was talking about them getting a divorce, and people still think she had an affair with that cop. I couldn't even go to the damn post office without getting stares."

Diana laughed. "You're being dramatic. Sure, people like to gossip, but it's not that big of a deal. Everybody's got problems. Sue Ann and David had to pay for rehab for their son last month. It's just small-town talk, and who cares what people think?"

"I care. I've got a business to run in this town."

"And you think Matt and Shelia getting a divorce has affected your business?" she asked with a laugh.

"Don't patronize me, Diana. I'm just saying, the whole divorce was a big hullabaloo, and Matt made Shelia look like a damn fool insinuating she had an affair. Then, it was finally over. They can't start it up again. I won't stand for it."

"You won't stand for it?" Diana asked with a skeptical look. "Besides, we don't know if Shelia had an affair or not. Even if she did, well, so what? I wouldn't be happy if I knew she had an affair, but it's not the end of the world. People make mistakes. It happens. People *have* had affairs before. It is what it is. And if they can reconcile, then I'm all for it."

"Well, I'm not all for it. I'm going to take care of this. After this trip, I'm going to make sure she's done with him, and she'll be fine."

"You're going to make her resent you if you keep pushing her. She's not a child anymore, and if you keep treating her like one, you're going to push her right out of our lives—and she'll take our grandchild with her. I mean it, William. If your antics keep me from seeing Amanda, I'm going to be madder than a wet hen."

"That's not going to happen. Shelia idolizes me."

"Well, a woman can only take so much," Diana said.

"Exactly. She can only take so much of that high and mighty *EX* husband of hers, and it's high time she move on and put him behind her."

Diana sighed. "God, you're a stubborn man."

William smiled. "Damn right."

"Let's just try to enjoy our trip," Diana said.

"You're right." He took a bite of steak. "This steak really is delicious, and you can't beat this view."

***

Diana downed her last gulp of hot chocolate and stood to get in line for the ski lift. "Come on, William. Let's get in line," she said, but William ignored her and walked away from the exit. She huffed and followed him. "William! Dang it. You're not listening to me again. I thought we were going to ride the ski lift."

"Sorry," he replied. "I just have to make a quick phone call, and then I'm all yours."

She shot him a dirty look, "You said no more work on this trip. You promised."

"I know, and I'm sorry, but this is important, Diana. Let me make this call, and then I'll be done with work for the rest of the day. Go get another cup of hot chocolate. Sit in front of the fire with your book. I'll be done in a jiffy."

Diana nodded, and William waited until she was at the snack counter before pulling out his cell phone. He spotted a chair in an isolated corner of the lodge and made his way there to make his call.

"Sorbo. It's me. You got any questions about the plan?" Though he was relatively alone, William still whispered.

He scanned his surroundings while the caller replied.

"Greer? Jesus. I thought I told you to do this alone."

William wiped sweat from his hands onto his pants.

"Fine. He's kind of a sonofabitch, but I guess that's fine. Just make sure everything goes like I told you. All the details are important."

He looked at Diana from across the room, and she was eyeing him suspiciously. He smiled and gave her a wave.

"Yes, you need to call him. It has to look like you're in this together."

He listened again.

"I don't know. Talk to him about whatever the fuck you normally talk about when you call him. Keep it casual. These are stupid questions. Are you a fucking moron?"

William glanced at Diana again. She was back reading her book.

"No. I've already told you. You won't be in much trouble—hell, probably not at all. I know the sheriff. He owes me a few favors. Besides, the payoff should be worth any issue you have, and we'll cut Greer in too. But if you chicken out on me now, Sorbo, I swear to God, I'll make sure your fucking life is over."

William felt the blood rising to his cheeks as his anger mounted.

"I don't give a shit about your nerves. Just get it done," William said.

He ended the call and wiped sweat from his hands again. Then, he took a deep breath, donned a smile, and rose to join his wife.

Chapter Sixteen

Steve Sorbo sucked in a deep breath of nicotine from his cigarette and exhaled a puff of blue smoke in the truck. His long, oily hair was fastened into a ponytail at the back of his head, but still, sweat poured down his back from his neck.

He was meeting Daniel Greer and Justin Hinder at a small park outside the city limits, and he was the first to arrive. He glanced at his cell phone again to see if Matt had called him back. He hadn't.

"Shit," he said. "I can't help it if he won't pick up the damn phone," he said aloud. "William's just going to have to get over it."

His mind wandered again, going over the plan that William had dictated. Though William had wanted Sorbo to carry out the plot all by himself, Sorbo decided he needed help. There were too many details, and Sorbo wasn't thinking too clearly these days. *Probably the meth*, he thought. *That shit's poison, but damn, I like it.*

He shook his head to refocus. He had already called William and told him he had asked Greer to help, but William didn't know that Greer brought in Hinder, too.

"Hell, William don't have to know everything. I'm putting my own ass on the line for this shit, and if I decide I need some help, well, it's my right to do it," he said, trying to convince himself that it was okay.

Just then, a red Honda civic rolled into the parking lot. Sorbo noticed that the back glass window was missing, and in its place, a black, plastic trash bag was taped around the opening.

The car parked, and Justin Hinder and Daniel Greer got out of the car and walked toward a picnic table underneath a large oak tree. Sorbo took one more puff on his cigarette, threw the butt on the ground, and opened his door.

When he reached the picnic table, Sorbo said, "What the fuck happened to your back glass, Greer?"

Greer laughed and said, "Oh, that? Old lady problems. You know how crazy bitches are."

Sorbo nodded and glanced at Justin. "Hey, Hinder."

"What's up, man?" Hinder replied. "Let's talk about the plan, but first, tell me how much money we're talking about."

Sorbo wiped his hands on his pants. "Ah. Straight to the point. Well, I'm not sure how much we're talking about here. William says he's going to leave a hundred thousand in the safe for me to have upfront, but I don't really trust him about that. I guess it really depends on how much money he gets from insurance. He says he's going to give me fifty percent of the insurance money, and of course, we'll all split that evenly."

"Wait a minute," Greer interjected. "If you don't trust William, then why the hell are we doing this? We putting ourselves at risk for something that might not bring us Jack shit?"

Sorbo shook his head. "Naw. It'll pan out. We'll get some good money. I'm just not sure how much yet."

Hinder sat down on the picnic table. "Danny's filled me in a little bit, but let me get this straight. William's hiring us to break into *his* house, take *his* money, and frame it all on Matt? Ain't Matt his son-in-law? And hell, I thought you and Matt was friends. I don't give a fuck, but that's some cold shit, don't you think?"

Sorbo reached into his pocket and pulled out another cigarette. "I don't really want to frame Matt. He's a straight dude—always been nice to me, even gave me a trailer at a good discount, but I owe William some money, and he's got some shit on me. I used to sell him pills. So, if I don't come through, well, William... anyway, it don't matter. I already told William I'd do it."

"Yeah, but I've been thinking," Greer said. "I don't like it. Matt's not like us. He's already got money—plenty of it. Everybody knows him, and people like him. He even goes to church and shit. There ain't no way he's gonna take the fall for all this. We supposed to just trust William about that? I mean, if this goes bad, then we're the ones on the line—sitting our broke asses in prison. William and Matt, they got money, and you know how it goes. Nobody ain't gonna mess with the rich fuckers. Hell, how do we know that William and Matt didn't plan this together? Get us to agree to it, go to jail, while they split the insurance money and leave us out completely?"

Frustrated, Sorbo bounced on his heels. "Matt don't know shit about this, okay? Trust me. I know him. He'd never agree to something like you just said. He's as honest as the day is long, so there ain't no way that Matt and William are in this together. And William, well, he knows all the higher-ups in the town—the sheriff, judges, a bunch of cops. He said we might get arrested, but we won't be in long. They'll arrest Matt."

Greer lit a cigarette. "I don't like it, Man. I ain't ever trusted no rich fucks, and now, you're expecting me to trust William. I don't owe William shit, and he ain't got nothing on me. Sounds like a lot of risk."

Sorbo huffed and yelled, "We're talking about a lotta goddamn money. Of course, there's a risk, but fuck, you can't make that kinda money doing the shit gigs y'all've been doing the past few years."

Hinder stood up. "Keep your fucking voice down. Look, the way I figure it, William's the one controlling all this shit. He's got the money, got the contacts, pulling all the strings. If we really want to pull it off, make sure we get paid and lessen the risk, then we tell Matt about the whole plan."

Sorbo's eyebrows shot up. "Tell Matt about the plan? What the fuck are you talking about? William's trying to set it up to look like he planned the whole gotdamn thing. Why in the fuck would we tell him about it?"

Hinder smiled. "You've got to calm down, Dude. You gonna have a heart attack. I'm just saying, we doing all the dirty work, we might as well have a rich fuck on our side, too. Chances are, nobody's going to believe that pretty-boy Matt would do something like this, so we bring him in, get his input, cut him in. Even if Matt admitted to being the mastermind behind all this, he ain't gonna be in jail long. He's too highfalutin. He takes the main wrap, uses his rich-ass privilege to make sure he don't get a long sentence, and we get a short B&E sentence. I've done a stint like that before. Ain't nothing to it. Then, when we get out, we get paid. William wouldn't even have to know we cut Matt in."

Greer nodded his head. "Yeah. I like that. Sounds like a win-win to me."

Sorbo threw his cigarette butt on the ground. "That ain't gonna work. Y'all don't know Matt. He ain't gonna agree to that shit. I've already told you, he ain't like that. He ain't dirty. He's straight—don't even smoke or drink. He wouldn't go for it."

Greer stood. "You're wrong. I don't know Matt, but every man has his price, and when he finds out what his father-in-law has in store for him, he'll probably do anything to get revenge. And taking a huge cut of money from William Carson is perfect vengeance."

Sorbo sat down at the table. "Fuck. I don't know. I'll see what I can do, but first, we've got to iron out the details about the night we're gonna do it. Even if Matt agrees to all this, he ain't going with us to break into the house. That's on us, so let's get all the particulars right." Sorbo looked expectantly at Greer and Hinder.

For a minute, the park was quiet, with only the sounds of chirping birds piercing the air.

"Well?" Sorbo asked. "Are you in or not?"

"Fuck it," Hinder said. "I ain't got nothing to lose, anyway," and he sat down at the table.

Sorbo looked at Greer. "Come on, Danny. You might not trust William, but you can trust me."

"Fine. I'm in," Greer said. "Let's talk about the details, but I'm serious about cutting Matt in. Call him."

"Okay," Sorbo said, and he exhaled a sigh of relief.

Chapter Seventeen

Diana took another sip of her chardonnay and smiled at William. "This is so relaxing," she cooed. "I don't know why we waited so long to do this, but the mountain air is refreshing. It makes me feel alive."

"Yeah," William said with a grin. "I agree. Maybe we should just move out here for good."

"And leave the kids in Mississippi? Lord, they'd hate us."

"Well, they aren't kids anymore, technically. You don't think it'd be good to start over? It'd be a blank slate. No more pressure."

"Pressure? What in the world are you talking about, William? I'm having a blast on our vacation, but I love our life, and I love our home. I'd never move this far away from the kids and grandkids. You're not serious, are you?"

"Naw. I guess not. I was just thinking about it. I guess it's just a fantasy."

"You sure have been acting strange on this trip. You sure you're alright?"

"Yeah. I told you I'm fine. I wish you'd stop asking if I'm okay."

"I'm sorry, but you have to admit you've been edgy. It's almost like you're nervous, and I can't, for the life of me, figure out what's going on in that brain of yours."

Just then, William's phone rang. He pulled it out of his pocket, looked at the number, and said, "I've gotta take this, Diana."

"No, you don't, William. We're on vacation. Let it go to voicemail. That's what I'm talking about. You've been distracted all week. Your body's here, physically, but your head is somewhere else."

"That's enough. I gotta take this," William said abruptly as he stood and walked into the house.

Diana sighed and took a big gulp of her wine.

"This is William," he said, answering the phone.

"Hey, William. It's Tommy. I hear you're on vacation, and I hate to bother you, but I'm afraid I have some bad news."

William sat down on the couch. "That doesn't sound good. What's going on?"

"Somebody broke into your house last night. Ripped your safe open and emptied it."

"Shit," William said. "Ripped it open, you say? So, the safe's still there?"

"Yeah. It's still there, but they got into it."

"Well, who in the hell did it?"

"Hell, I don't know. It just happened. We're gathering evidence. What do you want me to do with you being out of town and all? You want me to call Shelia?"

"Shelia's in Florida with that ex-asshole of hers. In fact, it's pretty damn convenient that he was out of town when this happened. Don't you think?"

"I guess I'm not following you, William. Whadda you mean?"

William took a deep breath. "I mean, that shithead divorced her, didn't want nothing to do with her, and now, all of a sudden, he takes her to Florida. And while he's out of state, my house gets broken into. Sounds like he's got a good alibi in my damn daughter."

"You saying that Matt had something to do with this?"

"Hell yeah, that's what I'm saying."

"Well, I don't know Matt that well, but hell, William, he don't need no money. You have a lot of money in that safe?"

"Only my whole goddamn life savings, Tommy. And with assholes like Matt Grant, it ain't about the money. It's about getting one over on someone. I'm telling you now. Matt's behind this, and I want you to arrest his ass as soon as he gets back to Mississippi."

"Shit, William. It's a little early for all that, but you know I'll look into it. I'll figure out who did this. In the meantime, you might wanna call someone to get over there and put in a new lock to secure the place up. The door was broken down, so I boarded the place up, but it ain't that secure. We finished bagging all the evidence this morning, so it's all clear now. I assumed there was money missing out of the safe, but at some point, I'll need you to see if there's anything else missing. Make me a list."

"Yeah, yeah, yeah. I'll do all that. Fuck. This is going to ruin Diana's trip."

"I know. I'm really sorry, William. Y'all gonna come home early?"

"Hell naw, I ain't coming home. I paid a fortune for this fucking trip, and I'm getting my money's worth. I'll call you when I get home."

"Alright. We'll be in touch. Sorry again, William."

William ended the call and sighed. "Shit, maybe I thew Matt's name out too early," he whispered aloud. His gaze traveled outside the sliding-glass doors at Diana, who was still snuggled up under a blanket, sipping her wine. "Fuck," he said to himself. "Here comes the hard part."

***

William adjusted his shirt and squared his shoulders before walking into the Sheriff's department. At the front desk, he barked out, "William Carson here to see Sheriff Tucker. He's expecting me."

The chubby receptionist smiled and nodded. "I'll let him know you're here. You doing alright, Mr. Carson?"

"I've been better, Sue. How's that new grandchild doing?"

"Oh, she's a doll, and I'm spoilin' her rotten, lovin' every minute of it."

"Yeah. Grandchildren are the best."

Sue picked up the phone and spoke into it, and then she addressed William again. "He should be here in a minute. You can sit down if you want."

"I'll stand. Thank you, Sue."

After a few minutes, Sheriff Tucker rounded the desk. "William," he said, sticking his hand out for a shake.

"Tommy," William replied.

"Good to see you," Tommy said. "Let's go back to my office."

In Tommy's office, William wasted no time in delivering his intention. "I want my ex-son-in-law arrested, Tommy. I told you he was behind this break-in, and I want him in jail now."

"Now, wait a minute, William. We can't just go around arresting folks because you want us to. There ain't no evidence that shows he did anything."

"Well, that just means he's good at covering his tracks. I don't give a good god-damn if you have evidence or not. If you don't have any, then find some, and if you can't find some, then make something up," William yelled.

"Shit, William. Keep your voice down," Tommy said. "Look. I done told you. It's pretty clear that Steve Sorbo did this, and we think he had some help from some buddies." Tommy looked down at the file on his desk. "A Justin Hinder and a Daniel Greer. We'll be arresting them today."

"I know Sorbo. He'll tell you that Matt put him up to this. So, I want you to offer him a deal to turn on Matt."

"How do you know what he'll tell us, William?" Tommy gave William a long, insinuating glare.

"Don't try to turn this shit on me, Tommy. I told you what I want you to do, and I swear to God, if you don't, I'll…"

"You'll what, William? Are you threatening me?"

William paused and took a deep breath. "You and I've been friends for a long time, and we've got a mutual understanding. I've got your back, and you've got mine. We've never had no problems before, but you and I both know that I can ruin your career in a New York second. I don't want to do that, Tommy, but I need this done."

Tommy was silent for a moment. Then, he took a sip of coffee from the thermos on his desk. "You might *could* ruin my career, but I know as much about you as you do about me. You wanna turn this into a battle, see who comes out better?"

William laughed, deep and loud. "Don't fucking play with me, Tommy. We start a war, ain't no doubt who's gonna come out on top. You don't know shit that everybody else don't already know, and here's the thing. They don't give a fuck. I am who I am—a hardass with money and connections. Sure, people respect me, but I've got that old-school respect. Not you, though. You're a public official—an officer of the law. I ain't on no pedestal, so I ain't got a long way to fall—not like you."

Tommy sighed. "Fuck, William. What do you want me to do?"

"I already told you—arrest Matt Grant."

Tommy ran his hand through his hair. "I don't think he had anything to do with this. You really want me to arrest an innocent man?"

"He ain't innocent."

"Well, if I do this, then I gotta know the truth—know what I'm getting in to. So, I'd appreciate it if you'd be honest with me." He paused. "Did you set this all up? Arrange this break-in so we could arrest your son-in-law?"

William stared at Tommy for a minute. "Let's just say that I wasn't surprised when I got your call about the break-in."

Tommy put his hands on his desk and shook his head. "Fuck. I'm going to hell."

"Well, I'll be right there with you. Now, listen up. Here's how I want this to go."

Chapter Eighteen

The room spun, and Steve Sorbo tried to focus on the walls to lessen his disorientation. It had been a month since he carried out William's plan, and he was pretty sure the cops were close to arresting him. It was all he thought about these days. William had assured him that he wouldn't serve a long sentence, but he still didn't trust William. His phone rang, and he squinted to identify the caller.

"Shit. It's Greer," he said aloud. He pushed the button to answer the call. "What's up?"

"I heard they're putting out a warrant for our arrest today," Greer said. "Fuck. I'm nervous, man. I can't believe you talked me into this shit."

Sorbo grabbed his pipe and took another hit. He exhaled and coughed.

"Hey! Hey, you fucking crackhead. Are you listening to me?"

"Yeah. I hear you. It's all good. Just stick with the plan. When they arrest us, we've gotta tell 'em that Matt arranged it all, and then, William's gonna make sure we ain't gonna be in there long."

"What about Matt? They gonna arrest him?"

"Well, yeah, I guess. That's what this whole shit was about—getting him arrested."

"But he's in on it, right? You said you told him about it, cut him in. So, he knows, and he ain't gonna throw us under the bus?"

"Yeah, yeah, yeah. He knows what's up."

"I swear to God, Sorbo, if you're lying about this shit, I'll murder your whole fucking family. I told you from day one that William Carson is a lying piece of shit, and if you didn't let Matt in on this deal to give us a contingency plan, then I'm gonna fuck you up."

"Shit, man. Before, you were the one telling me to chill. Now, it's you that needs to calm down. Take a hit, bro. Relax."

"Don't tell me to relax. I can't do hard time. I ain't made for it."

"Look. When they call me in, I'll just keep you out of it completely," Sorbo said. "I'll just say that I did it and that Matt set it all up. Will that make you feel better?"

"I guess. Hell, I don't know. You sure Matt's in on this? He knows you're going to blame him?"

"Yeah. I done told you. I got this. I'll blame Matt like Carson wants. They'll offer me a deal to testify against Matt, and they'll arrest him. But there ain't no real evidence that Matt set it up, so they'll drop the charges real quick. Then, when he gets off, everyone will be all good. It'll all disappear."

"It all sounds too convenient. Are you lying, or are you just fucked up?"

"Oh, yeah. Naw. I ain't lying, but yeah. I *am* kinda fucked up right now."

"So, Matt knows that we're gonna say he was behind this shit?"

"How many times you gonna ask me that? Yeah, yeah, yeah," Sorbo said. "He knows. William's gonna get us a deal so he can get Matt arrested, and Matt knows we're gonna say he was the mastermind, but they ain't gonna have enough evidence to convict him, so it'll all work out for all of us."

"But we're gonna have to testify against Matt?"

"Fuck if I know, man. I don't know how all this shit's gonna work."

"Well, don't you think we should get our stories straight—about that night and shit?"

"Naw. Like I said, I'll just keep you out of it. Anyway, I don't think it matters. Fuck. If you get called in on it, we'll just tell em' what happened. We just gotta make sure we keep William's name out of it so it don't look like he's behind all this. I'm just ready for this shit to be over. Fuck."

"Dude, when this over, you've really gotta put the pipe down. That shit's rotting your brain."

"Yeah. Whatever," Sorbo said. "A'ight. I gotta go. I'll holla." He ended the call and sat the phone down on the coffee table. "Shit," he said aloud. "Shit, shit, shit."

***

Sorbo wiped the sweat from his hands on his jeans and looked around the small room nervously. When the door opened, he jumped in startlement.

"Hi, Mr. Sorbo. I'm Sam Robinson, the detective on the Carson burglary case."

"Uh. Am I under arrest?"

"No. You're not under arrest—not yet, anyway. You're what we call a person of interest. Now, I know you know what this is about. Your friend William Carson's house was broken into, and we know you were involved, so why don't you make it easy for yourself and tell us your story? Things'll go a lot easier for you if you're honest with us."

"Well, yeah. I mean. I know about William's house, but I didn't do it. I was just a lookout."

"A lookout?"

"Yeah. I was just supposed to make sure nobody came to the house. Matt Grant asked me to be the lookout, and he said I'd get paid ten percent from the robbery if I just sat there and kept an eye on William's house."

"Okay. Let's back up a little bit. Let's start at the beginning—how you got involved in all this. Who approached you about it?"

"Matt Grant."

"Okay. Tell me about that encounter."

"I mean, well, Matt asked me to help him break into William's house a bunch of times—said he wanted to get William back for all the bad shit he'd done to him. I didn't think he was serious, but one day, he just showed up at my house. Had his daughter with him. She played in the yard while Matt told me all the details about the burglary."

"And what day was it that he showed up to your house?"

"I don't know. A few days before the break-in. I don't remember dates too good."

"Okay. Well, what were the details?"

"I already told you. Matt wanted me to be the lookout—to watch the house while he broke in."

"Matt was going to commit the burglary himself?"

"Hell, I don't know. He didn't say, and I didn't ask no questions."

"So, all you had to do was watch the house?"

"Yep."

"And what were you gonna get out of it?"

"I already told you. Ten percent. Matt said it'd be 45 grand."

"So, did you do it?"

"Do what?"

"Were you the lookout during the robbery?"

"Yeah. I mean, I didn't do nothing wrong. I just sat in my truck and looked at the house."

"Well, what did you see the night you sat in your truck?"

"I didn't see nothing, really. Well, I saw a van pull up—a white van, but that's it."

"And what about the money? Did you receive your ten percent?"

"Naw. Matt didn't get it to me yet."

Detective Robinson made some notes on a file, and then he looked up and smiled. "Okay, Mr. Sorbo. Sit tight. We need to check on some of these details. Can I get you something to drink while you wait?"

"Naw. Uh. Naw," Sorbo replied.

***

The next week, Sorbo was sleeping on his couch when he heard a pounding at his door. He sat up abruptly, looked around his trailer, and wondered where he was. *What the hell was that?*

"Itawamba Sheriff's department. Please open the door," a voice called out.

"Oh shit," Sorbo whispered as he scrambled to hide his drugs and his pipe. "Uh. Give me just a minute," Sorbo called out.

Finally, he opened the door a crack and saw a group of officers through the crack.

"Can I help y'all?" Sorbo asked.

"Hi, Mr. Sorbo. I'm Sheriff Tommy Tucker. I need you to come out her a minute, please."

"For what?" Sorbo asked. "What's this about?"

Sheriff Tucker shifted uneasily. "We have a warrant for your arrest. Now, if you don't come out, we're coming in, so let's make this easy, okay?"

Sorbo wiped sweat off his brow and opened the door. "A warrant for my arrest? What the fuck are you talking about? There's some kinda mistake. Call William Carson. This ain't right."

"Hey, hey. I'm about to read you your rights, but before I do, let me remind you that anything you say can be held against you in court, so you might wanna watch what you say."

"I'm telling you. This is a mistake. William said..."

"Hey," Sheriff Tucker yelled. He looked back at the other officers and then turned back to Sorbo and whispered, "If you know what's good for you, you'll shut the fuck up and quit mentioning William's name out loud in front of all these cops. Just come on out here and let us take you in. I'm sure William'll take care of all this in due time."

Sorbo's eyes darted back and forth, trying to decide his next move. Finally, he sighed and said, "Fuck. Okay. Let me put some shoes on."

Chapter Nineteen

Sorbo sat on the edge of his cot and stared at his shaking hands. *Shit,* he thought. *I need a hit. I gotta get outta here soon.* Before this, Sorbo couldn't remember the last time he had been sober, and he didn't like it. His brain felt scrambled, and he couldn't think straight. He had been sitting there for what felt like hours, trying to remember what he told the detective about the burglary, but he couldn't grasp the memory of it. *William better get my ass out of here,* he thought.

Suddenly, he heard an officer at his cell door, and he looked up expectantly.

"I'm going to escort you to one of our interrogation rooms," the officer said curtly.

Sorbo nodded and stood. *Maybe William came through, and I can leave this afternoon.*

The interrogation room was cold, and Sorbo shivered and sat on his hands to hide his quivering fingers. This time, when the door opened, Sorbo was so startled, he emitted an audible shriek, and he nodded as the detective entered.

"Good afternoon, Mr. Sorbo," Detective Robinson said as he sat down at the table and spread out a file on the table.

Sorbo couldn't speak. He wasn't sure his brain would allow the words to form, and even if he could say anything, he knew his voice would shake.

"We've been checking on our story, and it turns out that we've brought in a perp that has a white van, and according to cell tower pings, this man was in that area the night of the burglary. So, that part of the story checks out. However, we also checked your phone and your buddy Daniel Greer's phone. They both pinged at the scene of the crime, so we know that you were both there on the night of the break-in."

Sorbo just nodded.

"We know that your involvement was more complex than just being a lookout."

Sorbo nodded again.

"Before, you didn't mention Daniel Greer. Did you know that he was involved in this incident?"

Sorbo nodded.

"Mr. Sorbo, I'm on your side here. I know you didn't plan this, but I need you to be honest with me and tell me what happened so we can lay blame to the responsible party."

Again, Sorbo only nodded.

"Now, why didn't you tell me about Greer before?"

Finally, Sorbo spoke quietly. "Awww, shit. Greer is my friend. We been friends a long time, and I didn't want to get him in trouble, but hell, we ain't that good a' friends." Sorbo's voice rose, and a dam of words broke loose. "So, I'll tell you the truth. Greer has been wantin' to break into William's safe for a long time. He talked about it all the time, but this one time, we was on a fishing trip, and he said he knew how to do it—that he knew somebody that could get it done real quick. He said Justin Hinder had done this kinda thing before and that he was a pro, so he asked me to get in on it, I didn't want to, but I needed the money, so I went along with it, but I ain't taking the fall for all this. I ain't taking all the blame for Greer. He and Hinder did this, and I was there, but I didn't do nothing, and hell, I didn't get no money, either."

"So, you're saying that Greer and Hinder are the masterminds behind this crime?" Detective Robinson asked.

Sorbo closed his eyes. *What the hell did William want me to say? Fuck. I can't remember the plan now. Dammit.* "Yeah. Yeah. That's it. That's the truth," Sorbo muttered.

***

Sorbo had just settled back into his cell and covered up with the scratchy blanket when an officer arrived and told him that he had a phone call. Sorbo didn't realize that you could get phone calls in jail, and he didn't know who would be calling him, but when he entered the small, empty office, the temperature was warmer, and he was relieved to warm up a bit.

The officer pointed to a chair beside the small desk. "Have a seat. Pick up the phone and press line 2. I'll be right outside."

The officer left, and Sorbo sat down, took a breath, and picked up the phone.

"Hello," Sorbo said.

"You dumb sonofabitch. You're blaming this thing on Daniel Greer now? I don't give a fuck about Greer. It's Matt. You're supposed to say that Matt orchestrated the burglary. What the fuck is wrong with you?"

"William? Is that you? When you getting me out of here?"

"I ain't ever gonna get you out of there if you don't stick with the fucking plan. Every time they ask you a question, you tell a different story. Get your shit together. Matt. Focus on Matt."

"Look, man. They told me that they got evidence of Greer opening a safety deposit box at a bank in Amory two days after the whole shit went down. Hell, they even got the proof that Greer's son took a bunch of money out of it. When they told me that, I just kinda went along with what they were saying."

"I swear to God, if you don't get your shit together, I'm going to end you."

"William, I can't think. Hell, I ain't got my pills, and my brain's all fuzzy, and my hands are shaking, and I might be dying. You gotta get me outta here."

"Listen, you crackhead, piece of shit. When you talk to the detective again, you tell them that Matt is the one who told you to do this. I don't care about Greer. They know he was with you, but that's fine. Just make sure you tell them that Matt's the one who put it all in motion—and tell them that Matt has *all* the money, for fuck's sake. Do you think you can do that?"

"Yeah. Yeah. I can do that," Sorbo said. "And if I say that, then you can get me outta here?"

"God, you're a retard. Yeah. I can get you outta there after they arrest Matt, but you've gotta quit changing your fucking stories, you moron."

Click.

"William? You there?" Sorbo asked. Sorbo put the phone back on the receiver and sighed.

***

The next day, Sorbo was back in the interrogation room, but this time, Detective Robinson and Sheriff Tucker were both in the room. Sorbo was hopeful that this was a good thing and that William had worked on getting him out, but then again, William sounded pissed on the phone.

Matt. Blame Matt. Don't forget. It's all about Matt.

"Okay, Sorbo," Sheriff Tucker said. "Let me be straight with you. The cameras are off, so it's just us talking here. We had to arrest Greer and Hinder because we know that they were with you the night of the break-in, but we also know that Matt was behind this whole thing. William had his suspicions about Matt from the start, and we've been following up on that. Now, Matt was out of town when this burglary happened, but that's mighty convenient, and that doesn't mean that he didn't plan the whole thing out *before* he left. Now, we just need you to fill in some details for us. This is a big case, and you're one little fish in a big pond. Matt's the big fish. Now, we got the press meeting us over here this afternoon. William's giving a statement, and I'd like to know that I can put this whole thing to rest. So, here's what I need to know from you. I know you, Greer, and Hinder actually carried out the robbery. Under Matt's instruction, y'all broke into the safe, took the money, and left, all like Matt told you to do."

Sorbo nodded. "Yessir. That's right."

"Good. Now, what about the money? How did Matt get the money? Did you give him the money? Or was it Hinder or Greer? Who had the money, and who gave it to Matt?"

Sorbo looked down at the table. *Think, Sorbo. Think.*

"If Matt didn't get the money, then technically, he didn't do anything wrong," Detective Robinson said. "I mean, sure. He might've told y'all to do it, but if he wasn't actually a beneficiary of the funds, then this is all hearsay."

"He got it out of a culvert," Sorbo blurted out.

"A culvert?" Detective Robinson asked.

"Yeah. I wrapped the money in a plastic sack and left it in a culvert. Matt was supposed to come get it when he got back from his trip. And I left it all. We trusted Matt—trusted that he'd divvy out our cuts later, but he kept it all. He took all the culvert money."

Sheriff Tucker smiled. "Ahhh. I see. That's very helpful, Sorbo."

Chapter Twenty

The smell of chocolate wafted through the kitchen, and Diana glanced at the timer on the microwave. "Five more minutes, Amanda, and the brownies will be ready. They smell good, don't they?"

"Yep, Nonna. I can't wait. I'm gonna eat ten."

"You're going to eat one," Shelia said, and she gave Amanda a brief smile. "If your Nonna lets you eat ten, then you'll be spending the night with her tonight."

"Oooh. *Can* I spend the night, Nonna? Can I?"

"Well, I don't see why not."

"No, Shelia said. "You can't spend the night. You have to go to Kaitlyn's birthday party tomorrow, and I don't want to have to come over here and get you early in the morning."

"Well, I could take her," Diana said.

"Look, Mama. It's Pop. He's on the TV," Amanda screamed.

Diana glanced at the TV and threw a worried glance at Shelia. "Shelia, get her out of here. Now. I don't want her listening to this."

Shelia rolled her eyes. "Fine, but she deserves to know the truth." Shelia looked at Amanda. "Amanda, go outside and ride your bike. I'll let you know when the brownies have cooled off."

"But..." Amanda started.

"But nothing. No arguing. Go."

Amanda sullenly plodded out the door, and Diana rushed to the remote to turn up the volume.

Across the screen, they watched as a handcuffed Matt exited a police car and shuffled into the police station. Then, the camera panned back to William.

"It's devastating. I guess you never really know folks. I always thought Matt and I had a pretty decent relationship. Sure, there were a few issues that we didn't see eye-to-eye on, but I always treated him like family, and I was real upset when he and my daughter split up. But, never in my wildest dreams would I have thought that he was capable of something like this," William said.

"Are you confident that your ex-son-in-law is guilty?" the reporter asked.

"Yes. Unfortunately so. I'm a-hundred and ten percent that they got the right man. He'd been planning this for a long time. It's real sad, but I'm also glad to get justice."

"Piece of shit," Shelia said.

"Shelia! Language," Diana replied.

"What? Amanda's outside, Mom."

"I don't care. You shouldn't talk like that. It isn't lady-like." Diana turned off the TV, and when she returned to the kitchen, she took the brownies out of the oven.

"Well, I can't help it. The whole thing makes me sick. Who does that? Steals your daughter's inheritance? How selfish do you have to be to do something like that?"

Diana sighed as she came back into the living room and sat on the couch. "William's so sure he was responsible, but I still have my doubts."

"Why?" Shelia asked. "They obviously have evidence on him, Mama. They wouldn't have arrested him if they weren't pretty sure he was responsible."

"Still. Do you really think he's capable of something like that? You were married to him."

"Well, I was shocked, but I think the love of money will make people do some crazy, evil things."

"Yeah, but that's the thing," Diana said. "Matt didn't *need* the money. You and I both know how much money he made—he's very well off, and from what I understand, he had a good, continuous income. It doesn't make much sense."

"Well, who knows what he had planned, Mama. Besides, people who have money are never satisfied. Enough is never enough, and Daddy says that Matt hates him."

"I know. That's what your daddy told me, too, but I never thought Matt hated him. William's hard to get along with, but Matt's always been real nice to us, and if he hated your daddy so bad, why was he willing to get back with you?"

"He wasn't willing to get back with me, Mama. As soon as we got back from that trip, he dropped me like a bag of potatoes. You don't think that's weird?"

"Well, you said he wanted you to go to counseling. I thought that was a good idea."

"I don't want to talk to some stupid shrink, and Daddy didn't like the idea, either. I just think it's pretty dang convenient that all this went down while we were out of town, and when we get back, he comes up with an opportune excuse as to why we can't get back together. Too many coincidences."

Diana sighed. "I don't know," she said, glancing out the window at Amanda. "He's always been such an excellent father. My heart just breaks for Amanda. She adores him."

"Honestly, I'm glad he was arrested. If he can do that, then I don't know what he's capable of, and Amanda is better off without him."

"Oh, Shelia. You don't mean that."

"Yes, I do, Mama. And I don't like that you're feeling sorry for Matt, thinking he didn't do this. If Daddy said that Matt did it, then I believe Daddy, and you should too."

"Like it or not, your daddy has made a lot of enemies over the years, honey. A lot of people are jealous of the success he's built, and God knows I'll love your daddy until the day he takes his last breath, but he has a lot of questionable acquaintances. Those other men they arrested, they hung around here all the time, and they always made me feel uncomfortable. And Matt, well, he's always been so sweet to me—never made me feel uncomfortable—not a single time. He's always shown me respect, and I always felt safe knowing he was your husband. I didn't have to worry about you because I knew he'd take care of you. And now..."

"Oh God, Mama. You're making me sick with this. Can we please talk about something else?"

Diana smiled. "Sure, Honey. But promise me on thing. No matter what happens, don't talk bad about Matt around Amanda. That's still her Daddy, and she loves him, no matter what we may think about the situation. Don't be that kind of mama."

Shelia rolled her eyes. "I'll do my best."

Diana patted Shelia's leg. "Good girl. Now, go tell Amanda the brownies are ready. I'll get the ice cream."

***

Later that night, Diana made a glass of wine and settled in on the couch. William looked up from his laptop and smiled.

"Amanda all tucked in?"

Diana smiled. "Yep. She fell asleep before I finished the story. She was all tuckered out."

"Good. That's good. Shelia coming to get her tomorrow?"

"No. I'm taking Amanda to a birthday party tomorrow, and I'll drop her home after the party."

"Oh. Okay," William said, and his eyes returned to the laptop.

"William?" Diana asked.

"Yeah?"

"Can you put the computer down? I want to talk to you."

"About what?" He closed the laptop.

"About Matt," Diana replied.

"Not this again," William said.

"William, I'm really upset about all this, and I can't stop thinking about how it's going to affect Amanda."

"Well, that's out of our control, honey. And Matt should've thought about the consequences of his actions."

"But what if they're wrong? What if he's really innocent?"

"Diana, they have witnesses—people that all heard Matt say he planned this. I know you don't want to believe he's capable of something like this. I don't either, but it is what it is."

"But all those witnesses—well, let's be honest, William. They're not the most reliable sources. Those boys are on drugs. Anybody can see that."

"Drugs or not, they heard what they heard."

"I'm still not sure. I have a bad feeling about this."

"Well, you don't have to be sure. *I'm* sure, and that's all that matters. You're a woman, and you have so many emotions, it's hard for you to look at this rationally. Now, quit worrying about it. You just focus on baking and making quilts, and let me handle the manly stuff."

"Don't do that."

"Do what?"

"Patronize me—and treat me like I'm some silly, fickle woman. This is serious, William, and it affects a lot of people."

"You don't think I know it's serious? Hell, it was *my* money that got stolen."

"*Your* money? It was *our* money, and we have excellent insurance, so we'll get most of it back. But the money isn't the point. The point is that a man's life is at stake here—and that man is the father of your grandchild."

"That man is an elitist piece of shit who's getting exactly what he deserves," William replied, his voice rising.

"Now, don't get angry. I just want to know the truth."

"I don't want to talk about this anymore."

"William, do you remember when we were in Colorado? The days before the break-in, you were distracted, and you were taking phone calls... and..."

"What are you insinuating, Diana?"

"I'm not insinuating anything. I'm just trying to have a conversation with you. I know you never really cared for Matt, and I never understood that because, as far as I could tell, he didn't do anything wrong. He was good to Shelia—and great to Amanda. I really just feel like you never thought anybody was good enough for Shelia. And, I'm just saying, if you've done something just because you don't like him..."

"I see where this is going. Do you really think I'm capable of setting up an innocent man to go to jail?"

Diana narrowed her eyes at her husband. "We've been married a long time, and I know more than you think I do. In fact, I know exactly what you're capable of, and to be honest, sometimes, your arrogant disdain scares the hell out of me."

"That's about enough," William said coldly.

"Let me make it clear. I swear on everything that's holy, if you're condemning an innocent man to a prison sentence to satisfy some prideful vengeance, then I'll..."

Suddenly, William slammed his fist down on the coffee table. "God damn it. That's enough. There will be no more discussion about this. Let the police do their jobs, and stay the hell out of it." William blew out a deep breath and stood. "Now, if you'll excuse me, I think I'll go get a shower and head to bed early."

Tears filled Diana's eyes. *God forgive him,* she thought.

***

The next day, Amanda skipped toward the car, the pink gift bag swinging in her arms. "Come on, Nonna. We're going to be late," she whined.

Diana laughed and pushed the key fob to unlock the car. "Hold your horses, youngin.' I'm going as fast as these old bones'll take me. What present did y'all get Kaitlyn?" Diana asked as she started the engine.

"Some jewelry from Mama's store," Amanda replied. "Kaitlyn's going to love it. The last time she and her mama came into the store, Kaitlyn begged her Mama to buy her a necklace and bracelet, and her Mama said they were too high-end for a child, whatever that means. But when they left, Mama said her jewelry is perfect for kids and that Kaitlyn's mama was too much of a redneck to appreciate good taste."

Diana frowned. "Your mama shouldn't have said that to you. That's not very nice."

"Well, it's true. Kaitlyn *is* a redneck. She even goes hunting with her daddy, but I still like her."

"Well, I'm glad you like her, but please don't call her a redneck to her face, Sweetie. Some people don't like that term, and if you call her that, it might hurt her feelings."

"Okay, Nonna," Amanda said.

***

When Diana pulled into the Sanders' driveway for Kaitlyn's birthday party, her first thought was, *Gosh. Shelia's right. They are rednecks.* The doublewide trailer was nice enough, but Diana saw an old, rusty car in the front yard, and car parts littered the grass beside the trailer. When they entered the home, Diana felt guilty for her thoughts, so she immediately scooted over to Kaitlyn's mother, Tanya Sanders, and offered to help with the party arrangements.

Tanya looked overwhelmed, so she thanked Diana and asked her to put a cupcake on each plate around the table. Each cupcake was decorated in pink camouflage with a plastic buck placeholder accentuating the frosting, and as Diana passed out the sweet treats, she counted five deer heads on the walls of the living room. William liked to hunt, too, and Diana loved cooking with deer meat, but she never could get accustomed to the trend of decorating walls with animal corpses.

"Girls," Tanya announced. "There's pizza on the buffet. Grab one of those paper plates there beside the pizza, and make your plate. Then, have a seat at the dining room table. Cupcakes are on the table. Everyone gets one cupcake, and after we're done eating, we have some games set up in the living room."

"What about my presents?" Kaitlyn yelled.

"We'll do that last, honey," Tanya replied.

As the girls rushed towards the pizza, Diana stepped back to avoid the crowd. Then, Tanya came and stood beside Diana.

"I hope I ordered enough pizza. They're taking it down pretty quickly," Tanya said with a laugh.

"Oh, it'll be fine," Diana said. Then she turned to face Tanya. "I'm sorry. With all the commotion, I didn't introduce myself. I'm Amanda's grandmother, Diana Carson."

Tanya smiled. "Yes, ma'am. I knew who you were. My husband bought a trailer from Mr. Carson last year. Kaitlyn just loves Amanda. She says that Amanda's the prettiest girl in their class."

"Awww. Well, isn't that nice?" Diana said. "I'm guessing from the camo, that Kaitlyn likes to hunt?"

"Lord, yes. She's a daddy's girl, and she loves to do anything her daddy likes to do. I'm so sad that my husband, Tim, isn't here. He's a long-haul truck driver, so he's out on a haul this weekend, but we're going to have another little family party when he gets home."

"That's a good idea," Diana said, and her mind instantly swirled around Amanda and how much she adored her father. *If he goes to prison, it's going to devastate her,* Diana thought.

Diana was still lost in her thoughts when she heard yelling. She focused her attention on the table and was horrified to see Amanda yelling at Kaitlyn. "You don't know anything. You're just a stupid redneck!"

Diana darted over to the table. "Amanda! That's a horrible thing to say. Apologize to Kaitlyn this instant." Diana looked at Amanda, who had hot, angry tears in her eyes.

"I'm sorry," Amanda muttered.

Diana bent down and whispered in Amanda's ear. "Okay. Come on, Honey. I think we better go now." Amanda

245

stood and followed as Diana went over to Tanya. "I'm so sorry. I don't know what happened, but we're going to go ahead and leave. I don't want to ruin Kaitlyn's party."

"Awww. Y'all don't have to leave," Tanya said. "It's just kids being kids. They'll be best friends tomorrow."

Diana smiled. "You're probably right, but I don't want to reward bad behavior. Anyway, it was nice meeting you."

"You too," Tanya said. "Y'all drive safe now."

***

In the car, Diana was fuming mad as she buckled her seatbelt. "Amanda Nicole Grant, you know better than that. I just told you on the way over here not to hurt Kaitlyn's feelings, and I'll be if you didn't..."

She glanced over and saw tears streaming down Amanda's face.

"Oh, Honey. I'm sorry for getting so angry. I just don't understand why you were yelling like that. I thought you liked Kaitlyn."

A sob escaped Amanda's lips. "I *do* like her, but she told everybody at the table that my daddy was a thief and that he's going to prison," Amanda wailed.

"Oh. Ohhh, Amanda. I'm so sorry. I had no idea that's why you were upset. Come here." Diana unhooked her seatbelt and embraced Amanda. "I'm so sorry, Baby. I know you miss your daddy, and this whole thing is just horrible."

Amanda pulled back and looked at Diana. "Nonna, Mama said that Daddy did it—that he robbed from Pop and that he deserves to go to jail."

Diana's face flushed red, and she immediately felt anger toward Shelia. Tears flooded her eyes, and her heart fluttered. "Honey, this is an adult situation, and you're much too young to have to deal with all this, but you're a big girl, so I'm going to be completely honest with you. I don't know if your daddy did it or not. Some people think he did, but I'm not sure. I know your mama thinks he did it, but here's the thing, Sugar. Even if he *did* do it, that doesn't change how he feels about you. Sometimes, good people make mistakes and do ugly things, but no matter what happens, I know your daddy loves you very much. He's always been a good daddy to you, and I know it's hard to hear bad things about him, and as time goes on, you might hear some more bad things. But it's okay that you love him. You *should* love your daddy. And none of this is your fault, Baby."

"Thank you, Nonna," Amanda said.

•

"Okay. Now dry those tears. We still have a few hours before I'm supposed to take you home, so why don't we make a trip to Toys"R" Us? How does that sound?"

Amanda smiled. "That sounds fun. Do you think Kaitlyn's gonna be mad at me at school on Monday?"

Diana smiled as she buckled her seatbelt again. "No, Honey. Everything's going to be fine. You just tell her you're sorry again, and I know she'll forgive you."

***

Amanda bolted into the house, yelling, "Mama, look! Nonna bought me a new Barbie."

"Great," Shelia said. "Just what you need. Another freaking Barbie doll."

"Amanda, go up to your room and play with your new toy, honey, while me and your mama have a little talk, okay?"

"Okay, Nonna," Amanda replied, and she ran up the stairs.

Immediately, Diana turned to Shelia and glared at her. "We need to talk."

"What happened?" Shelia asked.

"Well, Kaitlyn said something about Matt to the other kids at the party, and Amanda yelled at her and called her a stupid redneck."

Shelia busted out in laughter. "Well, good for Amanda. That kid *is* a redneck."

"Shelia, this isn't funny, and that's not what I want to talk to you about. I'm more concerned about what *you're* saying to Amanda about this situation."

Shelia huffed. "Gah, Mama. We've already talked about this. I think Amanda needs to know the truth, and I'm not going to lie to her."

"I'm not asking you to lie to her, but she's just a kid, Shelia, and she's going to be getting it from all sides with this stuff. This is a small town, and everybody talks, so she's going to be hearing bad things about her daddy all the time. She doesn't need to hear it from you, too."

"Well, her daddy *is* a bad man, and I can't help that. I didn't cause all this. Besides, if Daddy has anything to do with it, Matt'll be in prison for a long time, so the sooner she accepts that he's not the prince charming she always thought he was, the better off she'll be."

Diana frowned. "After all y'all've been through, you really believe Matt's a bad man?"

"Sure as hell do."

"I swear you and your daddy are cut from the same cloth. I know how close y'all are, and I know you think like him, but I swear to God, you better listen to me, Shelia. I'm telling you now. If you poison that child's mind with bad thoughts about her daddy, then it'll come back and bite you one day. It may be twenty years from now, but if you keep her from him, she'll eventually resent you for it."

"I'm not keeping him from her. He did that himself."

"You know what I mean. Psychologically. If you discourage her from having a relationship with him in the future, then she'll hate you for it one day."

"I disagree," Shelia said. "And Daddy disagrees with you, too. Matt's obviously a criminal, and no daughter of mine is going to be associated with a lying, criminal asshole, whether he's her father or not."

"Shelia, think how you feel about *your* daddy. What if someone tried to turn you against him? How would you feel about that?"

Shelia stood up and scowled at her mother. "It sounds like *you're* trying to turn *me* against Daddy, but I don't have to think about it because *my* father did nothing wrong. Now, I appreciate your concern, Mama, but Amanda is my daughter, and I'll raise her how I see fit. So, no offense, but I'd appreciate it if you'd stay out of it."

Diana grabbed her purse off the counter and headed toward the door. "Disillusioning that kid is child abuse, Shelia. Plain and simple. And right now, I'm ashamed of you—you *and* your daddy."

"Mama, don't leave," Shelia shouted at Diana's retreating back.

The door slammed as Diana left.

Chapter Twenty-One

"Daddy, you have to do something about Mama. Every time I see her, all she talks about is Matt this and Matt that. She even called me a child abuser because I told Amanda that her daddy is guilty. I know she's a little girl, but she deserves to know the truth."

William sighed and wondered if he'd made a mistake in orchestrating this situation. "Your Mama's strong-willed. Just like you."

"I know, but I can't take much more of her lecturing."

"I'll take care of your mama," he replied. "But I don't want you to falter. I'm not sure how far this'll go, but if you're called to testify, I want you to be certain about whose side you're on."

Shelia giggled. "Oh, Daddy. You don't have to worry about that. I'm always on your side."

"Okay. Good girl," William said. "Now, I gotta get back to work, Sugar. I'll talk to you later. I'll speak with your mom. Have a good day."

"Okay, Daddy. Love you."

"Love you, too, Sheila." William hung up the phone and glanced at his watch.

Only one hour before his clandestine meeting with Sheriff Tucker and the district attorney, Tim Simmons. He thought this would be a simple feat, but the sheriff and the DA were hesitant to implicate Matt without evidence—though they made it clear that fabricated evidence was permissible. *I should've put this into more capable hands than Sorbo,* William thought. *Stupid crackhead. Can't keep his story straight for shit. It's obvious he's lying, and the damn politicians don't want the pigeonholing to be obvious.*

William opened his desk drawer and removed his flask. He took a sip of whiskey and weighed his options. He could manipulate Sorbo into saying whatever he instructed—as long as the dumb sonofabitch could remember what to say... the same was true for Hinder and Greer. They were all low-life trash, and they'd do anything to stay out of jail—if only for the opportunity to keep using drugs. The sheriff had Matt arrested, and now, William just had to make sure that Matt stayed in jail—and that the prosecutor could convict him. Then, Matt would be out of their lives for good.

He took a swig of bourbon. And now, he had Diana breathing down his back—suspicious of his involvement in this whole thing. Not that she really cared. She knew about his nefarious business dealings, and she never cared before—not as long as she got her designer purses and diamond rings. No, she was only concerned for Amanda's sake—like all parents, Diana's weakness was her children and her grandchildren. William just had to convince Diana that Matt was bad for Amanda and Shelia. *That shouldn't be that hard to do,* he thought. Then he shook his head worriedly. *Too many irons in the fire, though.*

***

William walked into the small gas station diner and looked around. *Good,* he thought. *I'm the first one here.* He ordered a cup of coffee and sat down at one of the small Formica tables. The place was vacant, except for the greasy-looking teenage attendant. On the ride over, William had figured out a way to solve his issues—as long as he could get the other parties on board.

Just then, he heard the bell chime over the door, and Sheriff Tucker entered the store. The sheriff nodded and walked toward him.

"Sheriff," William said.

"William." Sheriff Tucker frowned and said, "Why in God's name are we meeting out here in the boondocks?"

William chuckled. "Because Tim Simmons is meeting us here, too. You know how he is—didn't want anyone recognizing him—scared of the gossip."

The sheriff nodded and sat down across from William. "I don't understand what I'm doing here. I've already had Matt arrested, and there ain't much more I can do."

William smiled. "I appreciate you arresting the person responsible for this crime. I just want to make sure he stays in jail."

Sheriff Tucker shook his head. "Hell, William. You know I don't have no control over that. There's a lot of moving parts to all this. The judge sets the bond, and if this goes to trial, then the jury'll make the decision about his guilt. I've done my part."

"And I appreciate it, but Matt has plenty of money. He can make bail and be out next week."

"Well, that ain't my problem. Shit. Find out who the judge'll be and talk to him."

"I've done that, but I also want a backup plan—an insurance policy, so to speak, and I know how to make that happen, but let's just wait for Tim to get here before I give you the details."

"Whatever," Sheriff Tucker said, and he looked at his watch. "This better not take long, though. I got shit to do."

The bell over the door rang again, and a man wearing a black hoodie and sweatpants entered. He looked around suspiciously and walked over to their table.

William emitted a loud belly laugh. "What the hell, Tim? You look like you're gonna rob the joint. What's with the thug outfit?"

Tim Simmons lowered his hood and rolled his eyes. "I told you on the phone. I don't like this shit. I'm the district attorney, and it looks bad for me to be meeting with you. I'm up for reelection next year, and I can't afford any talk of blemishes on my character."

William laughed again. "Nobody ever comes out here, cept' the occasional hick and a few thugs—people that don't even vote anyway. Besides, in that getup, nobody'd recognize you. Have a seat. Y'all want some coffee? It ain't too bad."

Tim sat down and grumbled, "No. I don't want any coffee. I want to get this over with. Now, what's the deal?"

"Well," William said. "As you both know, my son-in-law orchestrated a robbery in which my life savings was stolen."

"Yeah, yeah, yeah. We all know about your plan to ruin your son-in-law's life. Get on with it," Tim replied.

William shot him a dirty look. "Easy now, Tim. Let's not forget that reelection you hold in such high regard. Now, as I was saying before I was so rudely interrupted, my son-in-law, who perpetuated a particularly heinous crime against me, has been arrested. However, I'm worried that his incarceration may be short-lived. First off, he'll meet bail—no matter how high it is."

"Then, I'll just argue that he's a flight risk," Tim said. "Jesus. We came all the way out here for that?"

Sheriff Tucker spoke up, saying, "I don't know who the judge'll be, but Matt ain't got no priors, and he's pretty much well-regarded around here, so I doubt any judge'll deny him bail—even if you argue that he's a flight risk. Hell, most people know that Matt's not the type to fly the coop. It ain't in his character—just like robbing someone ain't in his character." Tucker gave William a pointed look.

"Well, fuck," Tim said. "I can't control the judge's decision, and before you even ask—no. I'm not talking to a judge about this petty shit, William."

William held his hand up. "No, no, no. I wouldn't ask you to do that, Tim. I'll take care of the judge. Look. It's real simple. The way I figure it, the judge will definitely set bail, and Matt will make bail and get out, but I've heard from the grapevine that Matt's interested in hiring a hitman to take me out."

"What?" Tim said, flabbergasted.

"Yeah. I got it from a good source," William replied.

"Holy shit, William. This is getting out of control," Sheriff Tucker said.

"Let me finish," William said, raising his voice. "I've heard that Matt wants me dead, so let's just say, as a hypothetical, that Matt hires someone to kill me—a confidential informant, to be precise. If that said informant testifies, then would the judge revoke the bond?"

Tim nodded. "Yeah. That'd do it, but I don't think your son-in-law is stupid enough to go through with all that—especially hiring someone who'd talk to the cops."

William smiled. "Let me take care of all that. Tucker, I'll need your help with this."

"I done told you. I'm done, William. I don't want to be involved in no more of this shit."

William cleared his throat. "Tucker, I don't need to remind you about that unfortunate incident that occurred a few years ago, involving drugs... among other things. I'd hate for that information to come out."

"I'm sick of your shit, William," Tucker said.

"I know you are, Tucker, but this is just one more little favor, and Tim, I just need one thing from you."

"What?" Tim asked.

"When this all goes down, I need you there—at the bond revocation hearing. I'm pretty sure Judge Roberts'll have the case, and he's on the up and up—always has been. I can't touch him, but I also know that you and Roberts go way back. He respects you, so he'll be more likely to revoke the bond if you're the one making the request."

"You can't be serious, William. I'm the fucking lead attorney. I don't attend bond-revocation hearings. I usually send one of the newbies for that kinda shit. It'll look strange."

William narrowed his eyes. "No, Tim. It won't look strange at all. There's nothing weird about you wanting to make sure that a dangerous criminal—a man capable of murder—isn't capable of hurting anyone else. Putting someone like that away—well, that's a good win for you—something you can brag about when you're campaigning. And, on the other hand, if you do *not* focus on putting away this dangerous criminal, well, the general public *might* just see you as someone who is weak—who doesn't go after wealthy white guys like Matt Grant."

Tim rolled his eyes. "Fine. Fine. I'll be there."

William smiled. "Good. Now, let's work out the details."

***

"Nonna," Amanda yelled as she bounded through the door.

"Hey, Sugar," Diana called, and she put her arms out for a hug. She pulled back and inspected her granddaughter. "Ohh. I see you got your uniform dirty. I'm gonna have to spot-clean those grass stains. Did you have a good game? Did y'all win?"

Amanda smiled. "No, we lost, but guess what?"

"What?" Diana asked.

"Daddy came to my game!"

"Awww. He did? That's great, Honey. I'm so glad you got to see him."

"Yeah, and MawMaw was there, too."

"That's great, Amanda," Diana said.

"Yeah, but hopefully, that'll be the last time Matt and his skank-ass mama ever see Amanda," Shelia said as she came in and put her purse on the kitchen counter. She rolled her eyes. "He looked like hell, and his mama looked even worse."

"Language," Diana said.

Shelia huffed. "Sorry. Mama, you still got some of Amanda's clothes over here? I forgot to bring her a change of clothes."

"Yes," Diana replied. "Amanda, go look in my closet on the bottom shelf in that brown basket. There's a bunch of clothes in there. You just pick out whatever you want to wear. And put your uniform on the washing machine so I can get those stains out."

"Okay, Nonna," Amanda said, and she ran down the hall.

"Well, I think it's good that Amanda saw Matt," Diana said, watching Amanda run. "Honey, be careful. Slow down," she called. "And Matt's mama, too. It's good for kids to know their grandparents and love them."

"I know *you* think it's a good thing," Shelia said. "Anyway, I don't think Matt saw me. I was sitting with Rebekah Stewart. Do you remember her?"

"Yeah. I think so. Ain't her daddy Ralph Fondren?"

"Yep. That's her. Anyway, her husband works with someone who used to work with Matt, and she said that nobody believes Matt—that all his friends think he's guilty, and the only one who's sticking by him is his mama—and hell, I guess she doesn't have any choice since Matt takes care of her. She couldn't even afford to feed herself without Matt's help." Shelia laughed.

Diana shook her head and poured herself a glass of lemonade. "Heavens to Betsy, child. Sometimes, the things you say... if I closed my eyes, I'd swear it was your daddy talking. I don't know why, on God's green earth, y'all celebrate somebody else's failures. It's just un-southern. He was your husband, and he's the father of your child, for God's sake."

Shelia laughed. "I take it as a compliment that I sound like Daddy. Anyway, I only celebrate my enemies' failures, and anybody can be a sperm donor. He ain't a father—not anymore, anyway."

Diana wrinkled her nose. "Ugh. Don't use the word sperm around me. Gross. You want some lemonade?"

***

A week later, William came home grinning. He immediately went to the fridge and cracked open a beer. "Mmmmm. Smells delicious," he said. "What's for dinner?"

"Fried chicken, mashed potatoes, gravy, biscuits, and green beans," Diana replied. "You're in a good mood. You have a good day?"

He smiled and took a swig of beer. "I did. Very good. But I need to talk to you before dinner."

Diana shot him a serious look. "Okay. Is everything alright?"

William nodded. "Sure. Everything's fine, but it *is* serious. Let's go sit on the couch."

Diana dried her hands on a dishtowel and made her way to the couch. William sate beside her, set his beer on the coffee table, and turned to her, the smile replaced by a somber expression.

"What's going on?" Diana asked.

"Well, I don't want you to be alarmed. I'm fine, but there's something you need to know. You know Matt got out on bail, right?"

"Yeah. Amanda said he came to one of her ballgames."

William nodded. "Well, as it turns out, as soon as he was released, he was pretty busy scheming. He tried to hire someone to kill me, Diana."

"What?" Diana shook her head. "No. No. Matt wouldn't do that."

William picked up his beer and took another swig. "I wouldn't think so either, but he did. He hired an informant—gave him money and everything. They got it all on tape."

Diana put her hand to her mouth. "Oh, my Lord," she said. "Are you sure?"

"I heard the tape myself."

Tears formed in Diana's eyes. "I don't even know what to say."

"Me either. I don't know if they've arrested him again yet, but they will, and obviously, his bond'll be revoked, so the good thing is that he'll be in jail for a while—at least 'til the case goes to trial, so I'm not in any immediate danger."

"I just can't believe this," Diana said. "Are you sure that you…"

William put his hand up. "Don't, Diana. I'll be honest with you. I may have had some influence on his arrest for the burglary, but this has taken things to a whole new level. I knew in my heart that he was a malicious, bad man. I'm a good judge of character, so I knew it in my bones, but this is even beyond my imagination."

A tear dropped down Diana's cheek. "Well, goodness, William. I'm glad you're okay. If something happened to you, I don't know what I'd do."

William patted Diana's leg. "Like I said, I'm fine, but do you believe me now when I say that this man shouldn't have a relationship with our granddaughter?"

Diana nodded. "Yes. Of course. I know Amanda will be devastated, but if he's capable of murder, then I don't want her around him."

William nodded. "Yeah. She'll be upset for a while, but kids are resilient. She'll be fine, Diana. We'll all be fine, and with this new development, I doubt we'll have to worry about Matt Grant for a long time."

"I still can't believe it," Diana said.

"I know. You never know what people are capable of." William clapped his hands together. "Anyway, how about that supper? I'm starving."

Chapter Twenty-Two

Tim Simmons picked up the phone receiver and waited for his secretary to answer. "Hold all my calls, and when Jack Ford gets here, send him back immediately."

"Yes, sir, Mr. Simmons," his secretary replied.

Tim took a sip of his coffee, frowned, and opened the bottom drawer of his desk. "I need something stronger than this," he said to himself, and he removed his flask, unscrewed the top, and took a long sip. Tim was sick of William Carson and his demands. Sure, Carson had some dirt on him, but so what if it came out? If he continued prosecuting this case against Matt Grant so severely, he was sure he'd look like an idiot to the community.

There are literally drug dealers and pedophiles on our case docket, and I'm spending all my time and effort on a burglary charge against a guy who was out of town when the robbery happened. Jesus. How in the hell am I going to get reelected after this?

He took another sip of his whiskey. "Demand the maximum sentence," Tim said aloud, mocking William's words. "Who in the hell does he think he is? He ain't the fucking godfather."

Just then, Tim heard a knock at the door, and the door swung open. Jack Ford entered, carrying a briefcase.

Tim looked him over and rolled his eyes, noticing the wrinkles in Ford's suit.

"Uh... Hi, Mr. Simmons. You wanted to speak with me?" Ford stuttered.

"Yeah. Thanks for coming in. Have a seat," Tim said as he put his flask back in his desk. "I wanted to talk to you about the Grant case."

"Oh... okay. I uh... yeah..." Ford stuttered.

"How'd you manage to get that case, anyway?" Tim asked.

"Well, I uh... I heard about it, and I kinda just went by the jail, and I... uh... well, I guess I was just at the right place at the right time."

Tim frowned. "You're nothing more than a glorified ambulance chaser, Ford. In other words, you just showed up and managed to talk Grant into hiring you."

Ford smiled as if he had just received a compliment. "Yeah, pretty much."

"Well, let's talk off the record. What's your opinion on the case?"

"I... uh... well. Honestly, there ain't much to it. There ain't much evidence—just some he-said she-said kinda crap. To me, it's just an open and shut case, but I know William Carson really wants Matt to be punished for this, and I was surprised to learn that you were taking the case yourself."

"Yeah, well, I was surprised myself, too. Listen, between you and me, William's on my ass with this case. He wants a guilty verdict, and he wants the maximum sentence."

"I... uh... I... hope you're not suggesting that I throw the case. I mean... I can't... well... I don't think..."

"Calm down, Ford. I'm not suggesting that you throw anything, but I do need your assistance in tampering this whole thing down. This looks bad for our community—a standup guy like Matt Grant sitting in the local jail. People are talking about it, and honestly, William Carson's making us all look like idiots—including you."

"Me?" Ford asked, his eyes wide. "How do I look like an idiot? I've been doing my job, and I... uh..."

"Give me a break. You dropped the ball on that attempted murder charge. You didn't see it coming, and when the evidence was presented, you just sat there with your dick in your hand, stuttering like you're doing now. You really think that made you look like a prized attorney?"

"I... uh... well... it was obvious that the charge was just an excuse to..."

"And yet, you did nothing to stop it. Your client is rotting over there in a cell, waiting for a trial, which will take God knows how long."

"I... uh... well... I mean..."

Tim thought he noticed a faint smile as Ford stuttered, and suddenly, a realization hit him. "Wait a minute. Wait a damn minute. I thought it was strange that you didn't put up more of a fight about the bond revocation, but the longer this shit draws out, the more money you make. Isn't that correct?"

Ford actually smiled. "Well, I... uh... I mean, Matt's a wealthy guy. It's not like he can't afford it, and we all know this case is a bunch of bull, so there's no reason I shouldn't benefit from the work I'm performing on his behalf."

"Jesus, Ford. I swear to God. This whole fucking city is corrupt, but your deceptive ass might be the worst of the bunch."

Ford laughed. "Sounds like the pot calling the kettle black to me, especially considering you just all but admitted that William Carson's in your ear. I'm sure the public would love to know that you're being manhandled by some trailer-making thug who hangs out with drug dealers."

Tim slammed his fist on the desk. "Listen here, you slimy piece of shit. You're nothing but a fucking clown, and every lawyer in this town knows it. You're a drunk that only half-ass does your job, and you might be draining Matt Grant's money, but he's not stupid. Yeah, he's naïve since this is his first run-in with the law, but it's only a matter of time before he figures out that you're mishandling his case, and then your cash flow will end."

Ford put his hands up. "Alright. Alright. You're probably right. Just tell me what you want."

Tim cleared his throat and took a sip of his now-cold coffee. "I want Matt Grant to plead guilty—to accept a plea deal."

"What? You can't be serious."

"I *am* serious. Look, if he accepts a plea, then we can get past all this crap, and I can tell William that it was the only option I had. Grant will get a guilty verdict like William wants, but he'll get a lighter sentence, and I won't look like an idiot trying to put a businessman in prison for the rest of his life."

"Yeah, but what do I get out of all this? I mean… come on. You know, if this goes to trial, he'll get off. No one in their right mind would convict Matt on these charges, based on the evidence."

"Yeah, but you and I both know you're not going to make it to trial. You do all the grunt work, and then Grant gets smart, fires you, and hires an attorney who's actually competent. If he does get a not-guilty verdict, the next attorney's going to get all the credit for it—not you. A plea deal might not be a win for you, but it's not a loss either.

You get the credit for negotiating a lesser sentence, and you get to keep your money train for a while."

"I... uh... yeah... I mean... I see what you mean, but it'll never work. You don't know Matt Grant. He's adamant about being innocent, and this guy's got pride. There's no way he'll plead guilty. No way."

"Come on, now, Ford. You might not be a good attorney, but you're an amazing swindler. Surely you can talk him into it."

"I... uh... I don't think so. I'm serious. He's dead-set on proving his innocence—clearing his name."

"Well fuck," Tim said, and he opened his drawer. "Let me think. I need a drink." He took out his flask again, took a sip, and held it up. "You want a pull?" Tim asked Ford.

Ford smiled and reached down to his briefcase. "No. I have my own," he said, pulling out his own flask and drinking from it.

All of a sudden, Tim smiled. "Wait a minute. What if there was a way for Matt to plead guilty without actually admitting he committed the crime?"

Ford took another long drink. "An Alford plea? We don't do that in Mississippi."

"Says who?" Tim asked.

"Hell, I don't know. I just know that it's never been done—or if it has, I don't know about it."

"You're an idiot, Ford. It *has* been done—just not much. And just because it's rare doesn't mean it isn't possible," Tim said.

"Uh... Yeah, but the judge would have to approve it, and we've got Roberts. You know how he is. He prides himself on his integrity. He'll never go for it—he'll smell a rat."

"Let me handle Roberts. If I can get approval, do you think you can get Grant to agree to an Alford plea?"

Ford smiled. "Oh yeah. Sure. I can package it up real nice—tell him that it'll make this go away faster. You should see him. He's miserable in there—a blubbering fool, all the time talking about his sick mama and how he misses his little girl. Easy emotional blackmail."

Tim frowned. "You're a sick fuck, Ford."

"Touché. It was your idea. I'm just along for the ride."

Tim frowned again. "I guess you're right. Here's to hoping there's whiskey in hell," he said, and they clinked their flasks.

***

"I'm telling you, William, this is our only option," Tim said into the receiver. "All you've got is a line-up of crackheads who've told a hundred different versions of this story. There's no way a jury would deliver a guilty verdict if this goes to trial."

"What about a bench trial? Why can't the judge decide his guilt?" William asked.

"Because you've already exhausted that avenue. You can't get anything on the judge, and I'm sure not getting involved in bribing a judge. That could cost me my license, and I already told you I can't get any deeper into this."

"And I've already told you…"

"Enough, William. I'm done. If you think you can keep me from getting reelected, then have at it. Or if you want to spread some of my dirt, then so be it. Some things are more important than pride."

"This is bullshit, Tim."

"Look. I don't like it either, but I don't see any other option, William. Another thing you have to consider is your daughter."

"My daughter? What the hell does she have to do with this?"

"She's in the middle of the whole damn thing. She was on vacation with Matt when all this went down, and I know you've already told me that she'll testify that Matt was the mastermind, but do you really want her on the stand?"

"Why wouldn't I want her on the stand?"

"Hell, William. You know how this community talks. Everybody in town's talking about her parading that Tremont boy around at revival a couple weeks ago—and then marrying somebody else the next week. And shit, don't forget Greer had an affair with Shelia in the past, too, and putting them both on the witness stand would be a disaster."

"Now, wait a damn minute," William said, his voice rising. "That's her personal business, and that has nothing to do with this case. She and Matt aren't together anymore."

"I know that, but it doesn't matter. It goes toward her credibility. She ain't a credible witness. You and I both know it, but your suborn ass would make me put her on the stand either way, and any attorney worth a lick would tear her apart—even that idiot Ford."

"Yeah, but if we do a bench trial, it's just the judge listening. We wouldn't have to worry about jurors—people who've already formed opinions about Shelia."

"Fine. Is that what you want to do? Just keep in mind, neither you nor I can sway Roberts. He's as honest as they come, and hell, if I was him, I wouldn't deliver a guilty verdict with this measly case. I assume you still didn't find any dirt on Roberts."

"Hell no. He's clean as a whistle—damn deacon in his church and volunteers at the Salvation Army homeless shelter every damn week. He's a fucking saint. Just my luck that he'd be assigned to this case. There ain't no way you can get another judge?"

"No. I've read through all the case files. He dots every I and crosses every T. I can't find any reason to request a new judge, and besides, I'd look like an idiot if I suggested that Roberts had done something untoward. He's a god in this department."

"I don't give a fuck about you looking like an idiot, Tim. I just want Matt to go to jail."

Tim sighed. "Yeah. I know about your intentions. Look, with this option, Matt *will* go to jail, and he'll have a guilty verdict, too. That's what you want."

"Yeah, but for how long? I want him out of my life for good."

"For long enough. Shit, William. This has to end. Enough is enough. He'll go to jail, do his time, and hell, when he gets out, it's not like he'll want to come over and hang out with you—I think you've succeeded in getting him out of your life."

"I want him to suffer."

"Jesus fucking Christ, William. Let me just go on the record as saying that if Matt Grant gets murdered or beat in a little county jail, then all eyes are going to be on you. It won't be good."

"I ain't gonna have him murdered, you dumb son of a bitch. I'm just saying. I want him to be miserable."

"Hell, he *is* miserable. He *will* be miserable. If he accepts this plea, then he's going to prison—real, live prison—not a comfy, cozy cell in Itawamba County. He's your son-in-law. You know him. He ain't hard. He's going to be in there with murderers and rapists—real thug niggers."

Tim waited for a response, but for several seconds, he only heard William's breathing. "Okay," William finally said. "I guess that's better than nothing. Let's go with the Alford Plea, then. I'll approve of that."

Tim rolled his eyes. "I wasn't calling for your approval, William. I was just calling to keep you in the loop. And I want to make it clear that I'm done with this shit. That's it. No more favors. Don't call me the next time you want to exact out some family-fucking vengeance."

"We're done when I say we're done," William replied.

"No," Tim yelled. "I said that's it. This whole situation was fucked up, and I'm ashamed I had any part in it. But Karma's a bitch, William. I won't be surprised when *my* Karma arrives, but when yours comes around, I'll be thrilled."

Tim slammed the phone down on the receiver, sat back in his chair, and closed his eyes.

Part Three
Unpardonable Condemnation

Chapter Twenty-Three

At 4 a.m., Matt sat on the side of his cot, holding his head in his hands. It all felt like a blur. *How did this happen?* he thought. Everything was silent except for the sound of his cellmate snoring softly on the top bunk. *How can he sleep so soundly?* Matt wondered. Tim had been Matt's cellmate for a week now, but Matt had only said a few words to him. In fact, he hadn't spoken to anyone. He was frustrated and furious and depressed. It wasn't fair. Innocent people weren't supposed to go to prison.

Matt pounded his flimsy cot, and the metal springs reverberated, echoing a clatter through the eerily silent walls. Tim continued to snore, and Matt rolled his eyes.

Lord, I'm so angry. I don't know what to do, Matt prayed. *Please protect my Mama and Amanda.*

Matt sighed loudly and flipped his Bible open to the bookmarked page. Using his finger, he scrolled down the page to continue reading where he left off yesterday when he was interrupted by the guards performing a check. He continued reading Isaiah 41.

> 10 'You are my servant';
> I have chosen you and have not rejected you.

> 10 So do not fear, for I am with you;
>   do not be dismayed, for I am your God.
> I will strengthen you and help you;
>   I will uphold you with my righteous right hand.
>
> 11 "All who rage against you
>   will surely be ashamed and disgraced;
> those who oppose you
>   will be as nothing and perish.
> 12 Though you search for your enemies,
>   you will not find them.
> Those who wage war against you
>   will be as nothing at all.
> 13 For I am the Lord your God
>   who takes hold of your right hand
> and says to you, Do not fear;
>   I will help you.

After reading the passage, Matt closed his eyes. "I hope that's true," he said aloud.

***

In the chow hall, Matt grabbed his tray and found an empty table. After tasting the mystery meat, he frowned, placed it back on his tray, and took a bite of the cold roll.

"Yeah. That meat's terrible," someone said.

Matt looked up to see his cellmate, Tim, sliding in beside him at the table. Matt nodded and took a sip of his water.

"You always this quiet?" Tim asked.

Matt didn't respond.

"Okay. You don't have to talk to me, but I hate to tell you, Buddy, we're going to be spending a lot of time together, and in a place like this, it don't hurt to have some friends. But it's your call."

Matt looked him over, as if seeing him for the first time. He was tall and fit, and though his black hair was disheveled, a dimpled smile flickered through his olive skin. Matt noticed the edge of a tattoo, barely visible around the sleeve of his prison scrubs.

"You wanna see my tat?" Tim asked, and he pulled up his sleeve. "It's a devil dog. I was in the core. You look like a military guy yourself. You serve?"

"No," Matt replied.

"Ahhh," Tim said. "He speaks. I was beginning to think you were a mute."

"Naw. I just don't have much to say," Matt said.

"I feel ya," Tim replied. "I was like that when I first got here, and I can't blame you. You gotta be careful in here. Can't trust nobody—except me, that is. I'm the only decent fucker in here." Tim laughed.

Just then, a big black guy sat down across from Matt. "Hey, new kid. What you in for?"

"None of your business," Matt replied, flashing the man a dirty look.

The man smiled. "I was being polite. I know why you're here. I know everything. They call me 'the boss' because I run shit."

"Shut the fuck up, Tyrone," Tim said.

"No, you shut the fuck up, Tim. I know all about you and e'rbody else. This motherfucker robbed his father-in-law. They ain't find the money, either. He be bidin' his time 'til he get out, and then he gon' be a millionaire."

"I didn't do it," Matt replied. "I'm innocent."

Tyrone laughed so loudly, men at the other table turned and looked around suspiciously. "Yeah, right. In here, we all be innocent. You didn't rob nobody, just like I didn't use a machete on that asshole who fucked my sister over."

"I ain't innocent," Tim said, finishing his mystery meat. "I was a teacher, and I slept with my student. Point blank. It was a Stupid mistake, but you wanna hear what's really fucked up?" He continued without waiting for Matt's reply. "I got ten years for a consenting sexual relationship, and this murdering sonofabitch only got eight," Tim said, nodding his head toward Tyrone. "The justice system is bullshit."

Tyrone laughed. "It's all about who you know, boys, and I done told y'all, they call me 'the boss' for a reason. I be knowing people in high places, so you wanna keep yo' time here all nice and cozy, then y'all better treat me with some damn respect."

Tim rolled his eyes and looked at Matt. "Don't listen to him. He's full of shit. He did cut up some dude with a machete, but in here, he's harmless—a fuckin' joke with a big mouth and a little dick."

"Aight. I see how it's gone be, Tim. I'll remember that," Tyrone said.

Tim laughed. "I'm just trying to give my roommate the lay of the land, and he ain't gotta worry about you." Tim nodded his head to the next table. "See that table over there?" Tim asked Matt.

Matt nodded.

"That's the dudes you wanna worry about. Stay outta their way. They all crypts, and most of 'em are here for life, so they'll cut a motherfucker and not think twice about it since they know they're not getting out anyway."

Matt's stomach rumbled, so he exhaled, picked up the ambiguous meat, and popped it in his mouth.

***

After a while, Matt began to trust Tim, and it was good to have a friend to talk to. He learned that Tim got a degree in math after getting out of the marine corps, and he accepted a position as a teacher at a private school. And though he *did* have a relationship with one of his students, Matt thought ten years was a bit excessive. At least he was honest, and after all, Matt had been through, hearing someone be honest was refreshing.

Tim and Matt worked out together for an hour each weekday, and Matt lived for the exercise time, as it broke up the monotonous schedule of the day.

One day, when Matt was spotting his cellmate in the makeshift gym, Tim said, "Man, I've been thinking about it, and your situation is pretty unique. Your lawyer really screwed you over, and I wouldn't doubt if he was in on the whole plan."

"Yeah," Matt replied. "I thought the same thing, but then again, I thought I was just being paranoid."

"I don't think so," Tim replied. "I mean, in my case, yeah, my lawyer talked me into accepting a plea deal, but hell, I woulda been stupid not to accept it. They had all the evidence—text messages and everything. It's just that the judge decided to reject my plea deal to make a point—he wanted to make an example outta me. But with you, your lawyer talked you into pleading guilty when it was obvious that they didn't have any evidence to convict you."

"Yeah. Thinking back, it was a stupid move."

"Naw. I get why you did it. You were worried about your mom, and that shitty-ass lawyer was exploiting money out of you. But that's another thing—he shouldn't have been able to demand more and more money. And even after you gave him all that money, he didn't do shit."

"Yeah. It sucks."

"It *does* suck, but you should do something about it. You can sue him, you know."

"Sue him? I don't know anything about suing people. And wouldn't I have to get a new lawyer?"

"Yeah, but I bet there are tons of lawyers who'd jump on that."

"I just have a bad taste in my mouth for lawyers after this, you know? It makes me wonder if they're all shady. I don't know if it's worth it—all the trouble... going through all this crap again. I really just want to do my time and move on with my life."

"I get it, but if you change your mind, you should ask some of the guards about a new lawyer. They know who's legit or not. Besides, they all respect you. I've heard 'em talking about it—how they think you got set up. I know they'd be happy to help, if you asked."

"Thanks, Man. I'll think about it."

***

That weekend, Matt's mom was scheduled to visit him. She was bringing Amanda, and Matt was excited and terrified. It would be so good to see their faces, but he was nervous about what to say to his daughter. He had no idea what Shelia had told her.

He waited at a table in the visiting room, sipping coffee, though he didn't need the extra caffeine, as his hands were already shaking. Visitors were escorted in one-by-one, and he watched as kids embraced their fathers, some of the more violent offenders still handcuffed. Kids cried, and tears sprung to the eyes of some of the biggest, meanest men that Matt had ever seen. He smiled, thinking about it. Though he was nervous, he felt comfortable in the visitor room. Here, they all had mutual respect for each other.

Even the toughest men in the world loved their mamas and their kids.

He glanced around the room one more time, and then he spotted her. Her blond hair was curled, and she wore a beautiful blue dress. She was taller now. Tears immediately sprung to Matt's eyes as he thought about all the moments he had already missed.

As she took tentative steps toward him, Matt glanced behind her and saw his Mama. She smiled at him, and Matt noticed that she looked older, with more wrinkles. Her steps were slow, and she used a cane to assist her with walking. Her eyes twinkled, though, and he felt like a boy again, anxious to be in his mama's arms.

Amanda approached him silently, with fear in her eyes.

"Hey, Baby Girl," he said, putting his arms out for a hug. When she didn't come in for the hug, his heart broke. "It's okay," he said. "Come on. Have a seat."

Amanda sat down, and he reached for his mama, who squeezed him in an earnest embrace. "Oh, Matt. You look good, honey. I've missed you so much."

"Thank you, Mama. I've missed you, too. How you doing?"

"I'm making it just fine," she said, pulling away.

"You want some coffee?" Matt asked. "Amanda, you want a coke?"

Amanda shook her head, no, and his mom said, "No, no. I'm fine. I'm just happy to see you. Are you okay?"

Matt motioned for his mom to sit at the table. He pulled her chair out for her, and then he sat down and took a sip of coffee. "Yeah. I'm fine, Mama. I have a good roommate. Nice guy, and I've kind of started my own business in here." He laughed.

"Your own business? How does that work?"

Matt smiled. "Well, I'm up real early, so I go get coffee for people. A lot of people don't want to venture out if they don't have to, if you know what I mean." He glanced at Amanda, not wanting to mention any of the apparent dangers of prison.

His mom nodded.

"Anyway, I deliver coffee in exchange for extra desserts at meal time—stuff like that. The food's mostly horrible, so when there's something edible, I try to take advantage of it any way I can." He laughed.

"Well, that's good, Sweetie," his mom said.

Matt looked at his daughter, who was chewing on the fingernail of her index finger. "How's school, Amanda?" he asked.

She took her finger out of her mouth and looked down. "It's good."

"Have you been getting my letters?" he asked her.

"Yes," she replied.

"I've missed you so much, Baby Girl. I think about you every day."

She looked up at him, and he saw tears in her eyes.

"Oh, honey. I know it's hard to see Daddy in here like this, but I won't be here long, and when I get out, Daddy'll take you to do anything you want to do."

"Mama said she's gonna make it where I can't see you anymore, ever again," Amanda spewed out, and she burst into tears.

He reached over and patter her hand. "Don't worry, Baby Girl. That's not gonna happen. She can't do that." Then, he looked at his mom. "She can't do that, can she?"

His mother shook her head, indicating that he should drop it and not talk about it in front of Amanda.

"It's all gonna be okay, Honey. You look so beautiful. Is that a new dress?"

She wiped her tears and smiled. "Yes," she said. "MawMaw bought it for me, and she curled my hair, too."

"I noticed. You're gorgeous, Honey."

"Oh, Daddy," she moaned, and she sprung from her chair and ran to Matt.

When she wrapped his arms around him, he suppressed the urge to sob aloud. He closed his eyes and savored the moment, imagining he was home with her.

When she pulled away, she was back to her regular old self, beaming those precious dimples. "I love you so much, Daddy."

"I love you, too, Baby Girl. Hey. I've got an idea. You wanna see Officer Byrd's handcuffs? He's a good friend of mine."

"Yeah," Amanda said.

Matt motioned for Officer Byrd, who approached the table. "Hey, Byrd. This is my daughter, Amanda. Could you show her your handcuffs while I talk to my mama for a minute?"

Officer Byrd smiled at Amanda and put a hand on her back. "Sure thing, Matt." He bent down to Amanda's level and smiled at her. "You know what? I can also show you where we keep the *good* snacks. You like chocolate chip cookies?"

"Yes," Amanda squealed.

"Alright, come on," Officer Byrd said, leading her away.

"See you in a little bit," Matt yelled after her. Then, he turned to his mama. "What's this business about Shelia not letting me see Amanda?"

His mom exhaled loudly. "I don't know, really. It was just a rumor that I heard. For a while, I didn't hear hide nor hair of any of 'em."

"Did Shelia drop Amanda off at your house?"

"No. Diana brought Amanda over this morning, and she just said hello, but I didn't ask her about Shelia. Anyway, you know how our town works. About a month ago, I heard Shelia was gonna file for full custody and try to make it where you weren't allowed to see Amanda at all. And then, I got a call from Shelia last week, just out of the blue."

"She called you? What'd she say?"

Matt's mom shook her head and closed her eyes. "She said she still loved you—said that maybe y'all could work things out when you get released. I kind of ignored that and asked her about the custody rumors I heard."

"And what'd she say?"

"Well, as a Christian woman, I don't want to repeat the atrocities that came out of her mouth, but suffice to say, she pretty much told me that if you didn't take her back, she'd make sure you can't see Amanda."

Matt's eyebrows furrowed. "She can't do that, can she?"

"Honey, she probably can—especially since you pled guilty."

"But it was an Alford plea—it means that I'm not really guilty."

"I know that, Darling, but you know how bad off the family court is. They don't much care about fathers' rights, and from what I hear, it's pretty easy to get a father's rights terminated—especially if he's been incarcerated."

"Mama, I can't take Shelia back, but I don't know if I'll make it in here if Shelia takes Amanda away from me."

His mother patted his hand. "Honey, nothing's happened yet, and if I've learned anything, it's that you've gotta take life one day at a time. So, let's not focus on that right now. Amanda's here now, and she's missed you."

Matt nodded and took another sip of coffee. "Yeah. Lemme go find Byrd. We've got a little more time to visit before y'all have to leave."

Chapter Twenty-Four

The days were long, and yet, the time flew by. Days turned into weeks, and weeks turned into months. Matt realized how he took simple things for granted: sitting in a chair that had a back on it, the taste of ice cream, the beauty of green grass.

Day in and day out, the schedule was the same. Wake. Eat slop. Work out. Cleaning duty. Go to sleep. Occasionally, a fight broke out between gang members, and the prison would go into lockdown, but other than that, each day after endless day was the same. With what free time he had, Matt wrote letters, read books, and talked with Tim.

Amanda came to visit him a few more times before he received court papers, informing him that Shelia had been awarded full custody. His parental rights weren't terminated, but the judge granted an order for Matt to be barred from seeing Amanda—the matter would be revisited after his release. Still, he wrote her a letter every day, even though he couldn't mail the letters—the order maintained that he had no contact with her—even written contact—for *her* best interest. In his heart, Matt knew that cutting him off completely wasn't in Amanda's best interest.

The final straw that plummeted him into hopelessness was a letter from his uncle.

Hey Matt,

I missed seeing you at Thanksgiving this year. It just wasn't the same without you. I've been praying for you every day, and I'm looking forward to seeing you when you're released.

As you know, I attend the same church as William and Diana Carson. In the past, they didn't attend much, but since you've been in prison, they've become pretty active in the church.

Anyway, I always try to mind my own business and stay out of gossip, especially since I know you're not capable of the things they accused you of doing. But, I feel like it's my duty to tell you what's going on—or what I've heard's going on. I can't really confirm if it's true or not.

Basically, your Aunt Sue heard that Shelia has been taking Amanda to a highfalutin therapist. That, I know is true because I've heard William bragging about paying for it.

Anyway, Sue claims the therapist has convinced Amanda that you're guilty and that you're bad for her. Like I said, I don't know how much of it's true or not. I've seen Amanda at church with Diana a few times, but she wouldn't even look at me when I spoke to her.

But, in our small group Bible study last week, the teacher asked the group to pray for Amanda. He said that Amanda is 'estranged' from her father.

This, of course, puts me and Sue in a bad spot, and we just don't comment on it at all, but I do want you to know that we believe you, and we support you. I can't imagine what it feels like to be separated from your child, but I felt like you deserved to know what's going on, since you're getting out soon. I didn't want you to be blindsided.

Sue and I will continue to pray for you. We love you, Son, and we're looking

```
forward to seeing you when
you get out. Please take care
of yourself in there.

Love,

Uncle Jim
```

That night, Matt read the letter three times, balled up the paper, threw it in the trash, and cried himself to sleep.

***

Each day, Matt's depression grew deeper and darker, until he felt as if it would swallow him whole. His only reprieve from the obscurity of his situation came during his workouts with Tim and his new job in the kitchen, which at least occupied his mind, for a time.

One day, he got a surprise visit from his cousin, and in his heart, he knew it was bad news. *Please, God, let Mama be okay,* he prayed.

In the visitor's room, Shea gave him a sympathetic smile, and Matt said, "What's wrong? Where's Mama? Is she okay? What happened?"

"Sit down, Matt," Shea said.

"No. Just tell me," Matt replied.

Shea ran her hands through her hair. "She's okay, but she had a stroke. It was a small stroke, and she's gonna be fine, but she's gonna need some therapy. She's in the swing bed unit at the hospital right now. Depending on how well she does, she may get to go home soon."

"Damn it," Matt said, and he slammed his hand on the table.

Immediately, a guard approached them. "Everything okay here?" Officer Smith asked.

"Yeah," Matt said. "Sorry. My mom had a stroke."

Officer Smith cringed. "I'm sorry, Matt. She gonna be okay?"

"I don't know," Matt said, and he sat down at the table.

"I'm really sorry, Matt. I really am, but do me a favor. Please try not to have any more outbursts. You know the drill. If you cause a ruckus, I gotta move you outta here, and I don't want to do that."

"Yeah. I know. I'm sorry," Matt said.

Officer Smith patted Matt on the back and said, "Enjoy your visit. I'll be praying for your mama."

Shea sat down at the table and grabbed Matt's hand. "Mama and I are looking after her, Matt. She's tough. You know that."

Matt looked up at her with tears in his eyes. "Yeah, but what if she can't go home? What if they want to put her in a nursing home?"

"Well, the state'll pay for it, if they decide to go that route."

Matt shook his head. "Mama has always said that she doesn't want to be in a nursing home. She made me promise a long time ago that I'd keep her at home. She said she wants to die in her house. Besides, the state'll pay for some shitty place where she won't be taken care of. If she *has* to go into a facility, I want her in the best place available."

Shea nodded. "I know. I do, too. But she can't afford it, and neither can we. And, unfortunately, after all the money you spent on lawyer fees, you can't afford it either."

"This is bullshit," Matt said, raising his voice. He looked over at Officer Smith and lowered his voice. "I'm her son, so wouldn't it be my call?"

"Well, no. A couple weeks before Aunt Ann had the stroke, she granted Mama a medical power of attorney. Your attorney told her she needed to do that a long time ago, but she just got around to doing it."

Matt sighed. "Well, that's good that Aunt Jane can make the decisions about her health, but if y'all have to transfer her to a facility, make sure you let me know first."

Shea put her hand over Matt's hand. "We will. You know we'll keep you informed. Like your mama always says, 'Let's take it one day at a time.'"

"Well, whatever happens, don't let them take her to some shit hole. I'll figure something out, so if she does have to go somewhere, I'll pay for it."

***

The next day, Matt took Tim's advice and asked some of the guards if they could recommend a good lawyer to represent him in a suit against Jack Ford. And just as Tim predicted, the guards were happy to oblige. He made some calls, chose a new attorney, and set up a time to meet with his new lawyer.

The attorney he chose was professional, courteous, and efficient. By the time Matt had his first meeting, the attorney had already created a motion to present Ford with a settlement amount.

"I hate to tell you this, Matt, but you really were treated unfairly," John Grady said. "I've looked over your case profusely, and there was literally no evidence that you perpetuated this crime. I don't know a lawyer in the country who would have suggested you take an Alford plea on this case. I know you probably don't want to hear this now, but had you taken this case to court, you would've been found not guilty—without a doubt. I think your lawyer made a shady deal and got some kind of kickback for you pleading guilty—and I'm going to prove it."

Matt was both relieved and frustrated. "So, if you prove that my lawyer acted unjustly, can I recuse my guilty plea?"

"No," Grady said, shaking his head. "Unfortunately, not. When you're sentenced after a trial, you can file an appeal, but there's nothing to appeal in your case. Even though it's an Alford plea, it's still a guilty plea in the eyes of the law. But, you *can* get compensated for your trouble."

"Well, that's good."

"I've composed a motion to present to Ford, and it requests a prolific amount of money to settle. Of course, I know Jack Ford, and there's no way he'll accept this settlement. First of all, he can't afford it, and secondly, he's too damn prideful to accept it, but that's my intention. I want him to know that we mean business, and I want him to deny it because I'm eager to prove his misconduct."

"What about the lawsuit that William filed against me? Ford told me about it, but then, I didn't hear anything else about it."

"It's been thrown out. Like I said, they wouldn't have been able to prove that you committed this crime in criminal court, so they sure as hell can't prove it in civil court."

"So, what do I need to do?" Matt asked.

"Nothing much," Grady said. "I'll get you to sign these papers so I can file this motion, and we'll go from there. I'll take care of the rest."

"How much is this going to cost me? And how much do I have to pay you upfront?"

Grady smiled. "You pay me nothing upfront. I only get paid if we win the case, but don't worry, Matt. We *will* win the case. My fee will come out of your settlement," he said, taking papers out of his briefcase. "The compensation percentage and all the details are right here in this contract."

For the first time in a long time, Matt breathed a sigh of relief.

***

The next week, Officer Byrd came to Matt's cell and yelled, "Hey Grant, your lawyer's here."

Matt looked up from the book he was reading with a confused look on his face. "Really? He was just here last week. Didn't think I'd be seeing him again so soon."

Byrd shrugged. "I dunno. They just told me to come get you, but it must be important because he requested a private room. We set you up in the nurse's office so y'all can have some privacy."

Matt's stomach churned, and his mind raced with trepidation. *Great,* Matt thought. *Just when I thought things were looking up, here comes some more bad news.*

Matt followed Byrd to the nurse's office. Byrd held the door open for him, and when Matt entered, his stomach dropped even more.

"What the fuck?" Matt yelled. "What're you doing here?"

Byrd stuck his head in the door and spotted Jack Ford. "I thought you hired John Grady," Byrd said.

"I did," Matt replied, still glaring at Ford.

"Want me to get him outta here?" Byrd asked Matt.

"No. If you don't mind, I'd like to have a few words with him," Matt said, his voice low and full of menace.

"Alright," Byrd said, looking over at Ford. "But keep it somewhat civil, if you know what I mean. You're getting out soon, Buddy. Don't wanna mess that up."

"I got you," Matt said.

Officer Byrd left and shut the door behind him.

Ford put both hands up in a defensive motion and backed up to the corner of the room. "Now, wait a minute before you get all up in arms, Matt. I just came here to get you to sign some papers."

"What kind of damn papers do I need to sign for you?" Matt growled. "Our business is done. I fired you. Remember?"

"Well, I think that was a mistake. You don't know what might be coming your way after you get out. There may be more lawsuits thrown at you—maybe those thugs that were associated with the burglary. You need to make sure you have a good lawyer who's familiar with the case."

Matt took a step toward Ford, and he tried to back up more, his back hitting the wall. "I have a good attorney, *now*," Matt said.

"I did the best I could for you, Matt. You know how it is. Everybody was against you, and I got the civil lawsuit against you thrown out. That was good, right?"

"John Grady told me all about that. You didn't do shit to get that suit dismissed. They dismissed it because there wasn't any evidence, and you knew that the whole time… knew that I was innocent and that I wouldn't have been found guilty, and still, you convinced me to plead guilty."

Matt took another step toward him.

"You took advantage of my love for my mother to get me to accept a plea that benefited *you*. It didn't benefit me in the least because I'm still innocent, and I'm sitting in this prison for a crime I didn't commit. What did you get out of it? Did the DA promise to help you on a future case? Or is it worse than that? Did William Carson pay you?" Matt yelled.

"That... Those are some strong accusations, and they're not true. There... there..." Ford said, stuttering now. "There was no way of knowing whether you would've been found innocent or guilty. If you'll just sign this paper saying that I'm still your attorney, I'll be able to protect you from any other threats that may come your way."

Matt crossed the room and stood inches from Ford. "I've gotta give it to you. You've got balls to come here and ask to be my attorney again. I'd like to knock your ass out, but I won't because I'm not willing to jeopardize my freedom at this point, but let me tell you one thing. If I ever see your spineless, manipulating carcass again, I *will* hit you—even if it means spending the rest of my life in jail."

"Is... uh... is... that a threat?" Ford asked, his voice trembling.

"No. It's a promise," Matt said. "Stay away from me, and stay away from my family."

Ford's lip quivered, and he opened his mouth as if he was about to say something, but it seemed that he changed his mind, and he closed his mouth.

Matt reached over and brushed Ford's shoulder. "Like I said, you've got a lot of nerve, but if I were you, I'd accept that settlement agreement my new attorney sent over. I know it's steep, but I don't think you want John Grady looking into your private affairs, now do you?"

Ford looked down at the ground, silent.

"You don't have anything else to say?" Matt asked.

"I... uh... well..."

"I think we're done here," Matt said, and he turned around and walked out of the door.

Chapter Twenty-Five

After a few more meetings with John Grady, Matt was confident that he'd win the lawsuit against Jack Ford.

Luckily, Matt's mother was released to her home, but home health had to come and help her. He was anxious for his release so he could make sure she was being taken care of, and he still needed the money from the lawsuit to help her with bills—and to ensure that he could afford to put her in a nice place, if it ever came to that.

He couldn't get Amanda out of his mind, and he continued to write letters to her, which he bound with a rubber band and kept in a shoe box in his cell. He hoped to be able to give them all to her one day—just so that she'd know that he never stopped thinking about her—or loving her.

He continued working in the kitchen, which wasn't fulfilling, but it broke up the monotony of the day. He had become comfortable with most of the guards, and he had even told them the story about his arrest and sentencing. Most everyone he talked to agreed that the justice system had failed him.

One day, he was leaving kitchen duty, and as he approached the guard station to be patted down before returning to his unit, he saw Officer Shankster looking frantically under the desk.

"Hey, Shank. Can I help you find what you're looking for?"

Officer Shankster looked up, startled. "Shit, Grant. You scared me. I didn't hear you coming. Naw. I doubt you can help me. I'm looking for some money," he said with a smile.

Matt returned the smile and said, "Well, it's your lucky day. You know that highway out in front of the prison? Well, if you get on it and go north for about ninety miles, you'll eventually run into Industrial Park Road in Golden, Mississippi. I've got some money hidden there."

Officer Shankster's eyes widened. "What the hell are you talking about, Grant?"

"I'm talking about the money I stole. Hell, I'll even give you the address. It's 230 Industrial Park Rd. There's only one culvert under that drive. Now, don't worry. It's a county road, so there probably won't be anybody out there to see you. Go look in that culvert, and you'll see a garbage bag. It's got two million dollars in it. You can have it, just as long as you split it with my Mama."

"You're fucking with me, aren't you, Grant?"

Matt smiled. "Naw. Ain't you heard? That's what I'm in here for—stealing money and hiding it in a culvert."

***

The next day, Tim pulled Matt into their cell and said, "Matt, what the hell's going on?"

"What're you talking about?" Matt asked.

"All the guards are talking about you confessing to the burglary—said you hid the money in a damn culvert. Hell, I wouldn't be surprised if they haven't driven out there to check."

Matt laughed heartily for the first time in as long as he could remember. "I didn't confess to anything," Matt said, still laughing. "I just told Shank I have a nest egg stored away."

"Well, do you?" Tim asked, one eyebrow arched.

"Maybe," Matt said.

"You're shittin' me. This whole time, you've been adamant about being innocent, and after all this time I've spent with you, I know you. You wouldn't steal a dime from anybody—whether you hated them or not."

Matt's eyes twinkled in joviality. "You know me, huh? Come on, Tim. How well do you ever know someone? Aren't all people capable of foul deeds—even terrible, malicious actions? Maybe it was all an act—me pretending to be innocent. Maybe I *am* guilty, and maybe I *really* do have a small fortune stored away, courtesy of my disgusting *ex*-father-in-law. God knows he'd deserve it if I *did* steal from him."

Tim shook his head. "I ain't listening to this bullshit. You're just feisty because you're getting released next week—trying to stir up some drama before you leave. Make things interesting."

Matt laughed loudly. "Maybe so, but hey. You're getting released pretty soon, yourself. When you get out, you gotta look me up. We might could even go into business together. I guarantee it'd be worth your while."

Matt winked and walked to the chow hall.

***

The day of Matt's release, he felt like a normal human being for the first time in months. He went around the unit telling his fellow inmates goodbye, and though a few men were resentful of his release, most of them were happy for him.

"Don't be cutting anybody up," Matt said to Tyrone as he fist-bumped him.

"I can't make no promises, Grant," Tyrone said. "But for real doe, you can tell me the trufe now that you leaving. Did you do it? You got some money stowed away somewheres?"

Matt laughed. "I guess you'll never know," he said as he walked away.

"Aw, man," Tyrone shouted after him. "You gone do me like that? Come on, Grant. Shit. Inquirin' minds wanna know."

Matt was still laughing when he went to tell Tim goodbye.

"What're you so damn happy about?" Tim asked.

"Oh, I don't know—freedom. Smelling fresh-cut grass. Feeling rain splash down on my face. You know, the simple shit."

"Yeah. I know. I can't wait, myself. I know you got these assholes in here talking about your ass. Now, everybody thinks you're some damn genius mastermind sociopath who fooled all the guards into believing you're innocent. That's all I'm going to hear after you leave."

Matt laughed. "Sorry. I couldn't help myself," Matt said, holding his hand out for Tim.

Tim took his hand and pulled Matt to him in a brotherly hug. "It's been a pleasure."

"For me as well," Matt said, pulling away. "I didn't think you were the sentimental type."

"I'm not, and if you tell anyone I hugged you, I'll say you're lying."

Matt laughed. "I'm serious about looking me up when you get out. I'll be in the book," he said, still chuckling.

"I'll think about it. I might not wanna look you up. I'm tired of seeing your mug and listening to your bullshit."

"Well, I'm tired of hearing you snore," Matt replied with a smile.

Tim laughed. "Fair enough. Now, get the hell outta here."

***

The sun beamed down on Matt's face when he walked out the door, and he paused, closed his eyes, and raised his head up to feel the warmth of the sun for a minute.

When he opened his eyes, his heart skipped a beat. *I hope Amanda's here,* he thought. He searched the parking lot and spotted Shea leaning against her car—alone. He sighed. *No such luck,* he thought. *It was a good thought, anyway.* He felt despair rising in his throat, and he pushed it back down and forced himself to smile.

He approached Shea, and she gave him a big hug. "How does it feel?" she asked.

"You can't even imagine," he replied. "I took so much for granted. Never again."

"Well, what are we standing around here for?" she asked. "Let's go home. Your mama's waiting for you, and she made that chocolate cake you love."

"Ohhhh. Cake," Matt said. "I can't wait. And I can't wait to fire up the grill... eat a big, fat juicy steak... and maybe some pizza... ooh, and fried chicken."

Shea laughed. "Of course. Whatever you want. You deserve it."

Chapter Twenty-Six

Sitting rigid in his recliner, Matt sighed heavily and dialed his mother's phone number.

"Hello," she answered.

"Hey, Mama. How are you feeling today?"

"I'm having a pretty good day today. The physical therapist came by this morning, and I did all my exercises, so I'm tired, but I'm feeling pretty good. How 'bout you? How are you doing?"

"I don't know," Matt said quietly. "I miss Amanda."

"I know you do, Honey."

"And I'm out of trash bags."

"Well, Walmart's still open. Go get some."

Tears formed in Matt's eyes. "I don't want to. Whenever I go somewhere, I feel like everyone's staring at me and judging me. I don't want to leave the house, Mama."

"It's gonna take some time, Sweetie. You were in there for a long time, and I know it's hard to get out and pretend like nothing ever happened, but things'll get better. I promise you."

Matt wiped his tears. He didn't need to let his mama hear him this upset. With her health, she had enough to worry about. "You're right. I know you are, but sometimes, I feel like I'm still in prison—just a different kind of prison. I can't even speak to my only daughter, and people look at me like I'm a criminal. Hell, I guess I *am* a criminal. I might've taken an Alford plea, but I'm still a convicted felon."

Matt's mom cleared her throat and said, "Okay, that's enough. That's enough feeling sorry for yourself. It was a horrible thing, what you went through, and it's not fair. But, Honey, life ain't fair, and sometimes you just have to suck it up and move on. And to be honest, most of this is in your head. People ain't looking at you no different than anyone else. People have their own problems, and as bad as it sounds, you're not that important. So what, if you're a convicted felon? You're strong. You *will* bounce back from this. Not to mention, you're one of the smartest, kindest men I know. And I'm not just saying that because I'm your mama. Now, I want you to take a shower, get dressed, and go to Walmart. Don't sit around that house feeling sorry for yourself."

Matt smiled. It was good to hear his mom giving him tough love. He had been taking care of her since he got home, and it was difficult to see her so frail after her stroke, but hearing her lecture him reminded him of how strong *she* was.

***

A few months later, Matt straightened his tie and entered Bethlehem Baptist Church. Pastor Griffin greeted him with a handshake, then led Matt to the pulpit.

Looking out at the glaring eyes of the congregation, Matt's stomach did a flipflop, and he wondered what everyone would think of him—a felon, speaking in church.

No, Matt told himself. *You're here because you have a testimony, so don't let the devil get in your head.*

Matt swallowed hard, smiled at the congregation, and began to speak.

"As you may know, I'm Matt Grant, and first of all, I want to thank Pastor Griffin for asking me to speak to y'all today. And I also want to thank each of you for being here—for listening to my story."

Matt told them everything—starting from the moment he was first arrested to the glorious day when he was released. It was like it just poured out of him, and the more he talked, the lighter he felt.

"I don't want to take up too much more of your time," Matt said, "but I feel like I need to say this. We all have a story. As human beings, there is one thing that unites us all—and that is adversity. Life is hard. It's not easy for any of us, and no one gets out of here alive."

A soft chuckle echoed through the sanctuary.

"When I first came home, I felt pretty sorry for myself. It was hard to leave the house. I was used to having someone tell me what to do every minute of every day. And when I got out, the world seemed so large—so overwhelming, with more beauty than I could stomach... and the choices. I forgot how to choose for myself, and I was scared that every choice I made would be the wrong one. But going through that, I learned some important things. First, whatever you're going through, someone has it worse. You think you have it bad? What about that father in Alabama who lost his whole family in a car wreck last week? In an instant, his wife, his mother, and his two sons were gone.

"And so now, I look at the world through a new lens. I have a duty to be there for other people going through hardships—and sometimes, it may just be a kind word, a pat on the back, or a friendly smile. But pain—pain is universal, and by being there for your fellow man, you are praising God. He loves us so much, and love is the most important commandment for a reason—because it's powerful."

A few 'amens' rang out, and Matt smiled.

"Secondly, I learned that God never leaves us. He places people in our paths to help us through difficult times. Every time I got down on myself, someone was there to pick me up, and that's no coincidence. God shows his love through His church—His people, and I, for one, intend to live the rest of my life, allowing God to work through me. Now, I think y'all have listened to me ramble on long enough. Thank you again for listening."

As Matt stepped down from the pulpit, the crowd roared with applause, and Matt said a prayer of thanks.

***

Eventually, Matt's stomach didn't knot up when he had to leave the house. He stayed busy, though. He spoke at churches, and he was asked to join the community fire department, which took up a lot of his time. In just a couple months, he was promoted to the position of assistant fire chief. He won the lawsuit against Jack Ford, which gave him a financial cushion. Plus, before going to prison, he had a few rental properties, so he sold those, and he also sold the big house he had built for Shelia. The proceeds from the sales allowed him to start his own trailer business, where he could work flexible hours.

Every Tuesday, he had to check in with a parole officer, and though it still felt humiliating, it became part of his routine. His mother recovered from the stroke, but Time, the ultimate villain that He was, continued to advance, and as his mother got older, she required more of his time and attention for doctor's appointments, errands, and daily caregiving. He didn't mind. He was just glad to be home with her.

He never stopped longing for his daughter—to feel her little hand in his, to hear her high-pitched giggles. His parental rights were never terminated, but she wanted nothing to do with him. He considered going to court to ask for shared custody again, but he feared that forcing her to see him would do more damage to her than she had already endured. He reached out to her every week, and though he still had no contact with her, he was hopeful that one day, he could be part of her life again.

Chapter Twenty-Seven

William and Diana watched the sunset as they enjoyed a fried shrimp dinner on the marina's veranda.

"Oh, it's just beautiful tonight, William. Look at that purple streak over there."

"Yep. Sure is," William said as the waitress approached their table. "I'll have another beer, Hon," he said to her.

"Yes, sir. You need anything else, Diana?" she asked.

"No, thank you, Jenny. I'm fine for now."

"Okay. I'll be right back," Jenny said and scooted away.

"Look at all the yachts tonight," Diana cooed. "Why don't you buy me one of those?"

William laughed. "Yeah, right. I'll buy you one of those just as soon as you buy me a new Corvette."

Diana laughed and took a sip of her wine. "We've already talked about that. You're not allowed to have a midlife crisis."

Just then, David Artie approached their table. "Hey, William. How y'all doing tonight?"

"Just fine, David. How are you? How's Ginger?"

"Oh, she's good. She went to North Carolina this weekend to spend time with the grandkids. I guess I'm a bachelor tonight."

"Why didn't you go?" Diana asked.

"She ain't coming back 'til Wednesday, and I gotta work. You know how it is, William. Gotta make the money to make the wifey happy."

William smiled at Diana. "Happy wife, happy life."

"Well," Diana said, smiling. "Bachelor or not, you better be good, or I'll have to tell Ginger on you."

"Don't you worry about me. I'm spending the night on my boat tonight, just me and Jim Beam," David said with a laugh.

"I didn't know you had a boat," William said.

"Yeah. Had it for about a year now. It's high maintenance, but we really enjoy it."

"I bet," William said.

David took a big sip of his mixed drink and added, "In fact, we had a party at the yacht club last week, and guess who else bought a boat?"

"Who?" William asked.

David smiled mischievously. "Why, your favorite son-in-law. Matt Grant."

William's face darkened.

David pointed out into the marina. "There it is right there. That blue one. It's a pretty rig. Nice name, too." He turned to walk away, still smiling. "Good seeing y'all."

"What's the name on it?" Diana asked. "It's too far out. I can't see it."

"I can't read it either," William said, standing up and walking to the edge of the verandah to get a closer look. "Holy shit," he added a little too loudly.

"What?" Diana asked. "What is it?"

William turned around and frowned. "Culvert Money. He named the damn boat Culvert Money."

Epilogue

In 2014, Matt Grant entered an Alford Plea, which allowed him to plead guilty while still maintaining his innocence. Before Matt's case, an Alford Plea was rare, but since that time, the Alford Plea has been used more frequently.

Matt spent a year in prison. Though Matt considered many factors when entering an Alford Plea, one of the primary reasons for his decision was being able to serve minimum time so that he could care for his mother, whose health was deteriorating at the time of his arrest. A month before Matt was released, his mother had a stroke, which she thankfully survived, but the stroke caused severe paralysis. After Matt's release, he provided continual care for his mother, keeping her at home, just like he promised her.

After Matt was released from prison, Shelia still tried to get back together with him, but he never entertained the thought—especially since she had turned their daughter against him. Matt never rekindled his relationship with Amanda. But today, he still holds out hope that she'll reach out to him one day.

Daniel Greer, Justin Hinder, and Steve Sorbo were arrested for a short amount of time, but they were eventually released, and all charges against them were dropped. They served no prison time.

Matt reopened his trailer business, which thrived and is still in operation. Rumor has it that Matt's business is more successful than William's trailer business.

William Carson still lives in the same town, and he still owns and operates a trailer manufacturing business. The verdict is still out on whether he's still manipulating the local justice system.

Note from the Author

Dear Readers,

I'm often asked how long it took me to get back to normal after being sent to prison for something I didn't do. Well, the short answer is this: I'll never really be back to 'normal'—not that I was necessarily normal before. Now, I view the world through a different set of eyes. I witnessed what I believe is pure evil. I have seen and felt the corruption of the government. I felt powerless as I watched people, whom I once loved, blatantly lie. I have witnessed the two faces of society—the one on the surface and the other, hidden face—the one that lies in wait to ruin your life.

Before this situation, I searched for the good in all people and always had a smile for my fellow man. Now, I am more guarded. In my previous life, I would've tried to be courteous to everyone—even people I didn't like. But now, if I come across a person I don't care for, I choose to proceed silently. Honestly, I like this way better. I don't have the pressure to 'pretend' to be kind to unkind people.

At times, I still walk into a restaurant and feel people looking at me. Perhaps you've experienced a moment similar to this—when you enter a room, and the conversation around you stops. That's part of my life now—hearing whispers and seeing flitting glances, wondering if they're judging you.

For a while, it bothered me, but I'd like to think I've evolved. I've learned to understand human nature. Most people who claim to know me only know me in passing. They've never had a real conversation with me, though they've certainly never seen me do something illegal. Most people get their knowledge from the local news or, worse—from local gossip.

I've learned that many people are suspicious of me because they have the mentality that I must have done *something* wrong or the sheriff wouldn't have blamed me in the first place—the good ole' 'Where's there's smoke, there's fire,' mantra. In a way, I envy those folks—the people who still believe that judges see and know all the evidence before a trial—that all police, lawyers, and judges are just.

After I got out of prison, I stepped back into the trailer manufacturing industry, and it was easier than I anticipated. My ex-father-in-law had alienated so many of his clients, I had a large clientele as soon as I started. Since that time, business has grown exponentially, and I'm booming.

Early into this ordeal, I knew I wanted to write a book. After all, it's not every day someone is accused of the largest burglary in Mississippi while he's on vacation in another state. I feel like I owe it to the people who stood behind me through all this to let the truth be known.

Trust me. I've been over it a million times, wondering what I could've done differently, if any set of circumstances could have changed the outcome. As simple as it sounds, I could've made this all go away if I had stayed with Shelia—if I had blindly agreed to comply with her every demand. But life has taught me that 'what ifs' and 'what could've beens' are pipe dreams. Besides, if I had the option of a do-over—to stay with Shelia or endure the torture once again, I wouldn't choose her—not at the expense of losing myself. Through it all, my ethics never faltered, and I stuck with what I knew was right, and for that, I can look myself in the mirror, proud of the man I am.

Looking back, I think it has made me a better man, so for that, I regret nothing—well, except for losing the relationship with my daughter. Amanda still has no contact with me. This has broken my heart, and I'll never recover from it. She was my biggest consideration when questioning whether to fight in a corrupt court or to take a plea for a guaranteed one-year sentence.

I called and texted her for years after I came home, and during that time, I did get to see her twice. But ultimately, she believed what she heard about me—that I was guilty and that I mistreated her mother, her grandmother, and her grandfather. In the end, she was given a choice—to choose between them or me. She made her choice, and I don't hate her for it. I could never hate her. I'll love her until my last breath.

So, no. I'm not back to 'normal.' If 'normal' means having faith in today's society—in blindly trusting our judicial system, then I'll never be normal again, and I even consider it a compliment to be labeled an outcast in that regard.

I've written this book as a work of fiction, and I've taken some creative liberties, though the crux of the story is completely true. As a reader, you have the option to form your own opinions, to arbitrate a judgment of my character. Perhaps you've labeled me as a guilty man. You certainly don't know me, so I can't ask you to take my word for it.

As for me, your estimation makes no difference in how I live my life. I can only hope that this book provides entertainment and helps you to realize that everything isn't always black and white—correct or incorrect. The intricacies are in the details, and life is rarely fair or just. So, responsibility lies within us all—to make peace with the inner workings of our souls—to distinguish our own truths and conciliate our own principles.

I've done that. Have you?

Sincerely,

The Mastermind

> *But as for you, ye thought evil against me; but God meant it unto good*
> *Genesis 50:20*

Acknowledgements

First and foremost:
My Lord and Savior Jesus Christ
Also to the following:
My Mother Elizabeth Graham
Aunt Shirley Hill
Uncle Donald Fly
and the rest of my family and friends who
have stood with me through this.
I love you all.

And lastly, but not least:
All those wrongfully accused and those who our judicial system has failed.

About the Author

Matt Graham

Matt is an author, speaker, and owner of Masterbuilt Trailers. When he is not working he fills his time with old cars, motorcycles, traveling, skiing, fishing, and almost anything that involves the outdoors or nature.

Matt is a devout Christian and the third child of four siblings. Matt gives back to his church and a member of historical organizations. He prioritizes family and faith.

Matt is debuting his first book this year, based off of true life events, in which he reveals the mysteries behind Mississippi's largest burglary. Matt is planning on releasing the book in October of this year and pitching it for film. Matt hopes this book helps others understand the corruption of the justice system and show hope for those affected that they can have a future afterwards.

Future plans for Matt includes writing a sequel to this book and enjoying whatever life unfolds for him.

Made in the USA
Columbia, SC
14 November 2024